To Autumn

Katie M Hall

REVIEWS

"*Dirty Dancing*" for lesbians, swapping the Catskills for a caravan park in Devon, and Patrick Swayze for a lifeguard called Autumn. Katie M Hall effortlessly evokes all the angst of teenage lust and longing, making me both groan in painful recognition and wallow in delighted nostalgia. Catherine Hall, author of *The Proof of Love* and *The Repercussions*

"An impressive coming-of-age debut that weaves the electricity of first love with the raw ache of family fracture." Clare Lydon, author of the *All I Want* series and the *London* series

"Utterly charming and poignant. I think I have a crush on Autumn too!" -- Rosie Wilby, author of *The Breakup Monologues*

TO AUTUMN

KATIE M HALL

Affinity
Rainbow Publications

2025

To Autumn
© Katie M Hall, 2025

Affinity E-Book Press NZ LTD.
Canterbury, New Zealand

Edition First (1st)

ISBN: 978-1-991357-00-7 (paperback)

All rights reserved.

No part of this book may be reproduced in any form without the express permission of the author and publisher. Please note that piracy of copyrighted materials violates the author's rights and is illegal.

This is a work of fiction. Names, characters, places, and incidents are the product of the author's imagination or are used fictitiously and any resemblance to actual persons living or dead, businesses, companies, events, or locales is entirely coincidental.

Editor: Angela Koenig
Proof Editor: Lisa M
Cover Design: Fiona Ryan and Irish Dragon Designs
Production Design: Affinity Publication Services

Acknowledgments

Where to begin? So many wonderful people have been involved in supporting me to see To Autumn published.

Grandma and Georgie, your generosity has been the foundation holding me up while I pursue my creative dreams. You are with me always.

My MA course mates and teachers who read early sections and spent time providing invaluable feedback: David Vann, Gonzalo Garcia, AL Kennedy; Anna C, Anna L, Annie, Constanza, Dave, Ellen, Eve, Luke, Megan, Penny, Steve, and Vanwy.

The friends and family who gifted me places to stay and write: Mum & Davio, Jo & Elise, The Modern Literature and Culture Research Centre at Toronto Metropolitan University (Irene and Jason), Caitlin, Martine, Hazel, Denise & Jemma, Dad & Pat, and Tan & Ed. Thank you with all my heart.

My trusted beta readers, Tan, Jemma, and Heather: your confidence in the book enabled me to keep going every time I was ready to give up! And Georgina, whose hypnotherapy helped me over the finish line of the first full draft.

Fiona, who captured the heart of the novel and designed the epic cover art, way beyond my expectations.

To my editors Angela and Lisa, whose priceless notes and suggestions shaped the submission from draft to publication-ready. (Any stubborn remaining errors are mine alone.)

And finally, to Julie and Affinity Rainbow Publications, who took a chance and welcomed me into your lovely sapphic writers' community. I appreciate your support immensely.

DEDICATION

For Stan and Lou Lou, Pops and Moo, and Cally-bear. Dare to dream big.

TABLE OF CONTENTS

Chapter One	1
Chapter Two	14
Chapter Three	25
Chapter Four	41
Chapter Five	51
Chapter Six	67
Chapter Seven	74
Chapter Eight	85
Chapter Nine	90
Chapter Ten	103
Chapter Eleven	120
Chapter Twelve	133
Chapter Thirteen	144
Chapter Fourteen	149
Chapter Fifteen	159
Chapter Sixteen	167
Chapter Seventeen	175
Chapter Eighteen	178
Chapter Nineteen	188
Chapter Twenty	195
Chapter Twenty-one	201
Chapter Twenty-two	210
Chapter Twenty-three	218
Chapter Twenty-four	226
Chapter Twenty-five	237
Chapter Twenty-six	245
Chapter Twenty-seven	259
Chapter Twenty-eight	270
Chapter Twenty-nine	280
Author's Note	284

About the Author	287
Other Affinity Books	289

To Autumn

CHAPTER ONE

I pack up the crusty remains of the plastic cheese slice and pickle sandwiches Dad made us for lunch on the train. My little sister Anne and I are being sent away to Devon to spend the whole summer holiday with our grandmother.

I shove the mangled mess of dry crusts and crinkled foil into the tiny metal bin squashed between the backs of two turquoise upholstered seats. The lid squeaks open and shut, as if it's trying to rat us out - to whom, I'm not sure, as for now we are adult-free.

We have, of course, already finished the lunch box treats of Capri Suns and KitKat fingers (fours, not twos) that was meant to have survived beyond our never-ending train journey. I hand Anne a wet wipe to wash away the evidence that is smeared on her expressionless face and chocolatey fingers. I throw away the last of the wrappers and used wipes, and the bin squawks again, echoing in the hushed compartment. The ladies in the seats opposite us tut under their hats. The train's temperature is way too stuffy for wearing big hats, but maybe, like Mum always says, for some people appearances matter more than anything.

 I pull my best funny face at Anne, one that would have had her in hysterics before. She sees me but doesn't respond, and I'm left looking like a bit of a plank. At least it doesn't matter if anyone here notices. I promised Dad I'd try my hardest to be a good sister while we're away, but I'm finding it hard not to show how irritating Anne's constant silence can be. I don't know if I'll be able to stay cool with her for the whole six weeks. I mean, I appreciate it. I know how I'd be feeling if I was her, being sent away from home with just a geeky big sister for company while Mum's still in hospital. I just wish she would talk, say something, let me know she's doing okay.

 On top of everything, we definitely don't need strange ladies' disapproving tuts. We didn't need the fuss they made when we boarded the train because we have the reservation for the forward-facing seats. Too bad. Dad asked especially when he bought the tickets, because Anne becomes travel sick if she sits facing the wrong way, and I said no way would I be cleaning up any of that.

 A big yawn wins its way out of my mouth. I'm still tired after being woken up far too early by Dad this morning.

To Autumn

There was actual dawn birdsong when the alarm clock went off, something no teenager should have to deal with on the first day of their summer holidays, unless they're heading off on a plane to Disney World maybe. I wore my most convincing positive face when we left the house...well, I neutralised the face that could reveal how I really felt about waking up early just to be sent away. My face is always a dead giveaway of my feelings. Mum says she can read me like a book.

    I really struggled to keep up the conversation with Dad on the bus and tube we took to Paddington. My head was stuck in fantasies about being back in bed and having a lie in to celebrate no school for six weeks. The summer of 1997 is supposed to be one of the best of my life, at least that's what I was told over and over at school in the last few weeks of term. After we finished our GCSEs, the message from teachers was, "There's nothing you can do but wait for the results – and that's out of your hands until the end of August. Enjoy the freedom, things can only get better!" I had totally intended to channel their spirit, even though things didn't end up going quite to plan with my exams. I haven't been very successful. Life hasn't been easy or relaxing, with Mum in hospital and me worrying about how to tell Dad I've messed up my exams.

    Then, out of nowhere, Dad announced on Monday that Anne and I'd be heading off for the whole flipping summer without him. I think he deliberately left telling us to the last minute so that we wouldn't have time to talk him out of it. And now, instead of fun, the first day of the holidays began with climbing aboard a foreboding train at Paddington station, like something out of an Agatha Christie mystery.

From the platform, the train had an air of carrying important people to important places. Instead, it now carries Anne and me to our grandmother's holiday home, a caravan near somewhere called Newton Abbot.

I felt like Paddington Bear rather than Miss Marple, standing at the train door this morning, holding a suitcase and a plastic bag full of foil-wrapped quarter-square sandwiches. When Mum makes them, she cuts them into triangles and removes the crusts which is a bit more exciting, but today, just like the last three months, we're stuck with boring squares inside stale crusts.

Before the train set off, Dad stored our suitcases in the baggage rack. The cases are bulging with the new shorts, T-shirts, and swimsuits he shopped for us, and matching plain polo shirts very much in the fashion of "bought by a parent from BHS". We hugged him in the cramped compartment until he was told by the guard to wait on the platform if he wasn't intending to travel. He waved goodbye to us through the rain-stained window, trying to hide the fact he was crying – something we've all been pretending not to notice almost every day for the past month. He recreated his standard dad jokes, the old fake walking down steps, and holding his nose whilst making puffy cheeks and circles with his mouth to look like he was breathing underwater. I laughed along, even though, after the millionth time, the

To Autumn

jokes are no longer funny. I don't know why he thinks he needs to hide his tears.

Dad asked the train guard to keep an eye on us, and we were told very sternly by a nasally voice, "as long as you behave," we'd be okay. Everyone else in our carriage is a grown up; no other pairs of not-quite-sixteen-year olds and nine-year olds.

Dad's parting words after the suitcases were stowed were, "Robyn, look after your sister," passing me a baton of responsibility I haven't asked for and don't feel ready to accept.

In defiance, while I have my last few hours of freedom, I'm reading my magazines and listening to a compilation tape that was hastily but lovingly made by my best friends when they found out my summer sentence.

The tape is full of the Oasis tracks I love best. I turn the volume up loud on my new Walkman (a guilt gift from Dad), instead of looking out of the window and enjoying the stillness of field after field, which becomes more and more like a green carpet the farther away we travel from London.

I'm doing my best to ignore just how pissed off I am at the thought of being forced to spend my precious holidays in the middle of nowhere. Not only that, we'll be staying with Grandma, a woman we know only from stilted monthly telephone calls and birthday cards sent with five-pound Woolworths vouchers.

I could've been hanging out with my mates in London, trying to find some normality again after all the months of chaos and upheaval. From the moment we finished our last exams, my best friends Michelle and Tanith and I have been making intricate plans. They're supposed to be helping me find a boyfriend. Fantasies that made my heart beat faster, of hanging out at the Trocadero, sunbathing in Hyde Park, and watching fit swimmers at the lido are now just that – daydreams I'll be having, or worse, stories I'll be reading on the postcards they've promised they'll write. All I'm gonna have to tell them about is a summer of playing Uno and Pass the Pigs.

At least the sun's shining outside now. As the train pulled out of Paddington station, in the early morning drizzle, it felt like being sent away as a punishment but for a crime we haven't committed. The unfairness sits in my stomach like concrete, leaving no room for stale sandwiches.

Anne's barely looked up from her Barbie magazine all morning, while I can't concentrate on anything in my Smash Hits Summer Special, even the article on my favourite actress Winona Ryder, who I've not stopped thinking about since I saw her in *Beetlejuice* last Christmas. If only I could be Lydia Deetz and have cool surrogate ghost parents, then maybe things wouldn't be this hard and we wouldn't have to be sent away.

It's three months to the day since Mum drove her car into the red brick wall that surrounds Springfield Hospital. No one really knows what to do for you when your Mum tries to kill herself and ends up on a psychiatric ward in a special hospital for months and months. Dad's done his best.

He's managed to look after us and visit her every day and still make it to work every now and then. He was taking us to visit her every Sunday as well. We won't be able to do that from Devon.

I'm kind of relieved. I know it's my fault Mum did what she did. I know that's why she doesn't speak to me when we go and see her. Even though Dad says that she hasn't spoken to him either, I can tell he's lying about that. She must have told him what I did and that's why we're being sent away. To keep me out of trouble. That's why I need to find a boyfriend. It'll solve everything.

I've not told anyone, but the day before Mum drove into that wall, she walked in on me kissing someone on my bed. Not just anyone. Mum caught me snogging my friend Beth. It wasn't the first time we'd kissed, but it was the first time anyone had seen us. It was excruciating. Mum screamed at Beth to leave. After Beth left, Mum just sat at the dining room table rocking back and forth. Beth wouldn't talk to me after that.

The train starts to slow, and the view changes to yellow concrete and angry clouds. The guard announces our arrival at Exeter station. I've been told more times than needed that this means we are nearly there. The pit of my stomach starts to churn, like it is filling with expanding concrete. I try to settle it by whispering to myself as quietly as possible, "You can do this. You're grown up and strong. Anne needs you."

The two ladies with the hats shuffle and fuss as they stand up. The bigger lady catches her leg on the heavy black armrest.

"Blast!" she swears, then collects herself, and they both stomp out of the carriage.

The second lady makes a point of saying, "What an inconvenience. Thank goodness we can finally get off this blasted train," in a voice everyone can hear. She turns and gives Anne and me a long hard stare, almost crashing into the automatic-closing internal carriage door. "These modern doors," she cries, as they finish bumbling out.

A pleasant silence fills the air in their place. I wish that my only worry was trying not to stay stuck in the train doors.

After a few minutes, the train stutters and chuffs its way out of the station and no one sits down opposite us to replace those grumpy old women. There's no sign of the guard, so I stretch my legs and put my Doc Martens up on the seat opposite, fully aware of the lopsided poster above us advising passengers that seats are no place for feet. One perk of being adult-less. I shift back and forth in the seat, place my feet down on the floor, then up again, lean forwards and then back, picking up and putting down the magazine. The next stop will be ours, and it will be here very soon.

"Ants in your pants," I can hear Mum say in my head. She likes to use her weird phrases to describe people's behaviour. I used to find it annoying, but right now I really miss hearing those random observations. There hasn't been much laughter at home since she tried to end her life. That's how all the grownups describe it; they use euphemisms to make it sound less scary than she "attempted suicide" or "wanted to kill herself".

The coastline outside the window whizzes past. Why does time pass by at the opposite speed we'd like in a situation: too fast when we want it to go slowly and too slow when we want it to pass quicker. By this calculation, the impending summer will take a snail's pace.

I nudge Anne and ask her to start packing up her belongings into the Spice Girls rucksack she insists on taking everywhere. At least she has grown out of her Power Rangers phase. She looks at me fiercely, but after a pause she relents and sighs only half-gruffly as she stops her Walkman and puts everything away into her bag. I offer her a weak smile, trying to say, "hey, we're in this together," as the words won't come out. As usual, she doesn't say anything in response.

The nasal guard announces our imminent arrival at Newton Abbot station, signifying our fate of being signed, sealed and delivered to Devon; and perhaps also to the witch's cauldron I see in my mind every time I hear the word "newt" following months of revising *Macbeth* for GSCE English Lit. My stomach tightens even more, and I stop myself heaving by counting to five.

Dad's voice sounds out of nowhere in my mind. "You'll be okay, you're spending the summer with your gran and she loves you. Everything'll be alright."

We stand up and I'm sure Anne can see my hands shaking as I pull our heavy suitcases off the baggage shelves and drag them to the main carriage door. I fight with the window to jiggle it down to make sure I can reach the lock, as Dad showed me this morning. Was that only a few hours ago? Finally, it wriggles loose, and then all I can see is the platform in front of us.

†

We hear her before we see her, as we step down from the train.

"Annie! Robyn! Hellooo!" shouts a creased voice, emerging from post-box-red lips, and accompanied by a waft of warm floral perfume.

"She prefers Anne, Gran," I say, jumping in as peacemaker before Anne has a chance to react.

"Grandma, please," say the lips, while stencilled eyebrows peer around to make sure no one else has heard my faux-pas.

"Grandma. Yes. Of course." The foundation layered face and heat-set perm in front of me has Dad's nose and chin, which surprises me. I blink back some tears, but I can't shift the lump in my throat.

"These are our cases," I say, trying to sound perky and helpful, as I cough the words around the mountain lodged behind my tongue.

"Excellent, let's see if we can make them fit in the car, shall we?" Grandma walks towards an old burgundy Ford Fiesta parked in the taxi rank.

The car looks about as sturdy as a used baked-bean can might if it had wheels. The rust-edged coat doesn't do anything to disguise how old and worn out it is. The song we sang in middle school about rusty old cars "I'm just a little pile of tin, nobody cares what shape I'm in" worms into my head. I try to hide my disbelief that this car will be able to hold all three of us plus two heavy suitcases and our straining-at-the-seams rucksacks without collapsing.

"She's a top little runner, this one," says Grandma as if she can read my thoughts. "I've had her since new and she's never done me wrong. Not quite been the same since we had to change her to unleaded, but she gets me about."

I smile. I hear Mum's voice saying, "Always be wary of people who refer to their cars as 'she'."

"You've really looked after her."

"I think Annie should sit in the front," Grandma continues, snapping me out of the memory, "that's the only other seat with a belt." This is good news, because Anne's tendency for travel sickness applies to cars as well and she's better up front. One battle I don't need to fight.

Apart from when Anne was little, we haven't really been all that close, until this year. Because of the age gap, our lives don't usually overlap. But even though she hasn't said a word out loud since April, my big sister protector instinct keeps kicking in, and I wish I could make it easier for her, going through this. I've had to do a lot of babysitting the past three months, but I don't feel like I've been able to connect with her. Maybe being together here, away from the messiness of home, will give me a chance to show her I do love her. I'm sure there'll be things to bond over.

"Okay, I'm happy to sit in the back!" I say. I call upon on my well-practised Tetris skills as we pack the car, lowering the double backseat down and pushing the two suitcases forward. The boot just about closes and although I end up wedged between the bags and the car door, it means that at least it doesn't matter there isn't a seatbelt for me. There's no way any amount of force could throw me out of this position. Grandma fires the engine and then launches the car into rapid acceleration followed by a stop short behind another car at the exit, and I'm glad that I am wedged in between the luggage, fixed in place.

"Shouldn't take more than twenty minutes, loves," Grandma says just as we lurch out of the car park and onto a busy road. I shut my eyes. If I can't see the hazards that jump out from the Cycle Proficiency test highway code book, then I can't be frightened by them. Grandma doesn't know that we haven't been in a car since Mum's accident.

†

Finally, the Fiesta pulls into the long Smugglers' Cove Holiday Park driveway and slows down. There're a couple of billboard posters alongside the curb, with brightly coloured photos of happy kids having fun by the pool, in beach dunes, jet skiing, climbing in an adventure playground, and playing table tennis. Maybe the summer won't be a bust after all. The idea of some sun and swimming, my daily dose of *Saved by The Bell* and *Neighbours,* and hopefully a decent selection of magazines at the holiday park store, gives me a faint hope that we may survive our extended trip after all. I might just be able to do some of the things I'd been looking forward to in London. I hadn't thought about the possibility that there might be other families with kids my age here at the park on their holidays. Perhaps I'll find a boyfriend after all.

Chapter Two

"Where's your caravan, Gran...Grandma?" I ask as the shuddering car cuts into my daydream of sun, tanning, buff bodies, and chilled fizzy drinks.

"It's not a caravan. It's a static mobile home."

Who knew there's a difference? I picture a rustic log cabin situated on the edge of a tree-fringed lake that I now expect to be our home for the next two months. We pull up outside a custard-coloured corrugated shell, adorned with an orange awning and concrete slab steps. There's no lake, no log cabin; just rows and rows of other identical mobile homes. I can see us ending up lost for days trying to find Grandma's amongst all the others.

To Autumn

We load up with our bags and Grandma places the keys precariously on my little finger. She announces that she must go and park the car in the designated car-park area.

"You two are sharing the twin room with the bunks, I hope that's okay." Sharing? Dad most definitely did not mention this nugget in his sales pitch.

I'm not sure who gets the worse end of the bargain, Anne or me? I don't want to be in such proximity to my little sister, or anyone for that matter. I need my own space and privacy. What about when I dress, what if she's in there? I don't want her seeing my body. What if she snores? This sucks.

"Okay," I say, swallowing the lump again, "I'll unpack." We step up to the door and I unlock it. It swings open, almost knocking me off the step.

"Mind the door, dear," says Grandma without turning around, "it's heavy and swings fast. You should put the handle in the latch, and then it doesn't close on you." She drives off, thankfully sticking rigidly to the well-signposted, five-mile-an-hour speed restriction. I lug our two big suitcases up and into the large – for a caravan – lounge area.

Cream and peach bench settees, accessorised with matching curtains, form the edge of the room, up to a small dining booth that leads into the galley kitchenette. There are tiny cupboard doors everywhere. A small door opposite creates the sense of a hallway, leading off to two other doors. I can see that the far end, all of five steps away, leads to a double room, not the room for us. I try the nearest closed door, and it rattles on the hinges. It opens to a tiny room with bunk beds on one side, a closet rail and shelf at the far end, and a gap that I can only fit in standing sideways on.

"This must be us!" We cram in, Anne, me and the suitcases. Doing anything more than turning around in a tight circle is going to be an achievement in here. I send Anne to the sofa while I unload the contents of the bags into the tiny wardrobe and chest of drawers.

"Just put the TV on or something," I shout to Anne. There's no response and after a few moments I step back into the lounge area to see her opening every cupboard. It takes me a second to realise there's no TV set on display.

"It must be in here somewhere," I say in the most forced cheery voice I can muster. The concrete in my stomach tightens forcefully. "Oh, please no..." I whisper.

I scan the room five or six times, opening all the cupboards, looking under cushions, for any sign of a TV. I find a drawer full of photos of Grandma looking much younger, standing next to her sister, Aunty Di, and holding a toddler that could be me. The caravan is in the background, I can tell because it looks exactly the same in the photo as it does today. It shocks me to see photos of my life I didn't know about. I don't remember ever visiting Grandma and Di. We don't have copies of these photos at home – there are none of Grandma there, at least none Dad's ever shown me. These are the only photos of me in the drawer, and there aren't any of Anne, but then Anne certainly hasn't ever been here before.

However, no sign of a TV. "I don't think there is one," I admit, defeated. "Perhaps just read your magazine instead?" I return to the unpacking and counting along with the carriage clock that ticks by each passing second.

✝

I fold the last polo shirt away into the narrowest wardrobe I've ever seen and hear clumpy footsteps coming from outside. Grandma's back.

"We can put your cases in the storage space under the mobile home. You won't be needing them for ages, will you? And I suppose you'd like a tour of the site?" she asks. This is the first sensible thing anyone has said to us all day, and I feel a small drop of excitement and curiosity. My chance to see whether there's a possibility of fun, at all, ahead of us.

"Yes!" I exclaim, speaking for both myself and Anne, who is miles away in her own world under her headphones. See, it might not be all bad, is the message I try and give Anne through just a look. I take her hand and pull her up off the sofa.

At the bottom of the entrance steps, Grandma shows me where she hides the spare key, under a big beach shell.

"I don't think you will need it, as we'll be together most of the time, but just in case."

Together most of the time? I'm used to roaming free, away from the eyes of my parents, or anyone else for that matter. I've been taking the bus on my own since I started high school. For the last few summer holidays, I'd barely seen my parents. They trusted me to go off without them on the condition I checked in occasionally. That suited all three of us.

The sky has cleared a little, showing us a little bright blue behind white-rather-than-grey clouds. Grandma strides through the neat row of homes.

"These are the resident owned and occupied homes. Those over there are for the weekly holiday makers." She points to scruffier caravans on the far side of a rough pathway. Some kids cycle past us.

"I wish I had my bike," I say.

"Most of the time, the young people riding their bikes are a nuisance. I've petitioned to the managers of the park about banning bicycles from the site, or at least the areas near the homes," is Grandma's response.

"Oh." I must be showing my disappointment because Anne squeezes my hand in solidarity, rolling her eyes with bravado. We don't always need words to know we have people on our side.

We walk on, and after a couple of minutes of dodging bikes, mobile homes, children and pets, we reach what Grandma calls the centre of the site. Does that mean on the other side, there is another never-ending series of mobile homes?

"Here are the toilets and showers," Grandma says, as we approach a large single-storey block surrounded by oversized, metal sinks. "They're supposed to be for the tent campers but if you need a number two, I'd rather you did it here than in the home. Saves me having to pump the waste away as often. Nasty job. And if you want a long shower or to wash your hair, please come over here as well. Really, it's the best place to wash up dishes when there's several people's worth, and you've seen, it's just a short walk from my home."

This sounds like information we're being given for a reason. I can add washing up to the list of things I'm not looking forward to over the next six weeks.

Just as Anne starts to give me a funny look, Grandma spots her. "Well, Annie, no need to pull a face like that now, is there? Don't be soft, now. Surely, you've both been helping your father with the housework?"

"Let's see the rest of the park," I jump in, hoping to distract them both.

I march forward, towards the sound of splashing and a strong smell of chlorine, pulling Anne with me. Swimming is the only activity Anne and I enjoy together. Mum always says it must be in the genes, but Dad says it's because she taught us both as soon as we could walk.

We stop outside the turnstile. "Can we go in?" I ask, trying not to sound too excited as I've come to expect my hopes are going to be instantly dashed.

"You can have a look, but I'm not sure how often you'll be able to use the pool. I'm no swimmer, and the rules stipulate children must be supervised by a competent adult."

If I can't swim in this pool, there's a chance I'll go mad.

"But I can swim really well. I've passed my Grade Seven. Anne's nearly at Grade Five, even she doesn't need supervision. Mum lets us go to the leisure centre pool on our own."

"Rules are rules, Robyn. This is where I spend my summer months, every summer. I'm not prepared to be evicted because you two want to break the rules." I stifle my sigh into a yawn.

"No sulking, now, that certainly won't be tolerated. You two aren't going to be hard work for me, are you?" I look at Anne. We both turn to Grandma and shake our heads. "Good, I don't want to have to report to your father that you've been misbehaving. That's the last thing he needs after your mother..." Her words trail into a haughty silence.

"After Mum what?" I ask, daring Grandma to continue.

"After her…accident. Let's just all agree to be nice, do what we're told, and behave. Then everyone will be happy. Do we think we can do that?"

We? Who does she think she is, the Queen?

"Fine."

†

We walk through the metal gateway, and into another world. My body relaxes as the smell of chlorine wafts up my nose. The heavy concrete lump in my stomach starts to shrink now we're inside a space that feels familiar and comfortable, full of splashing and laughter. The three of us

To Autumn

stand awkwardly around the edge. Grandma stays very close to the tall wooden fence that closes off the pool area from the rest of the holiday park, but I'm eager to dive right in.

I never thought I'd be happy to see an ordinary scene of families, young kids, babies in rubber rings, toddlers in orange inflatable wings, children Anne's age jostling down a red slide. I was beginning to forget what ordinary is. I'm not even annoyed by all the screaming.

There's a large splash followed by an even louder whistle from the top end of the pool.

"No horseplay or you'll have a time out," a golden voice says, in an accent that could have stepped right out of Ramsay Street. I look up to see it accompanies expressive round eyes, shoulder length, straight, coal-black hair that rests neatly on broad sun-kissed shoulders, framing a dark olive complexion atop long, toned, tanned legs – just like the Olympic swimmers I've watched on the telly. She can't be more than a couple of years older than me, but she is unquestionably in charge here.

She is wearing a red one-piece swimsuit with the Smugglers Cove logo sewn onto the right breast. She walks back up to the tall white plastic seat which is positioned in front of the "Lifeguard" sign.

I can't move. My feet are stuck to the wet tiles. My heart stops beating. My lower jaw feels as though it has dropped to the floor. My palms sweat, and just like Mum teases me about, blood rises to my cheeks, betraying everything that is going on inside my body.

21

Something about the way this girl blows that whistle, the way she is yelling at the kids who were running at the lip of the pool, and the way they follow her command automatically and stop, the way that swimsuit flatters her physique, strikes me. Have I just been hit by invisible lightning? I could happily melt right into one of the puddles at the side of the pool. Everything else disappears, and it is just me and her. Who is this goddess?

"Onwards. I've saved the best to last. The entertainment hall and shop," Grandma says, snapping me out of my daze.

What is going on? My legs are jelly as I turn around and face Grandma and Anne. "Sorry, what?"

"Pardon me, I think you mean?"

I nod, not knowing what I am agreeing to.

"Chop, chop. Let's move on, finish the tour." Grandma and Anne walk towards the turnstile. Although it feels like wading in treacle, I manage to follow them.

As we bumble out of the turnstile, the whistle sounds again, stopping my heart for a millisecond, and I fight all my urges to turn around and go back to where I can watch the lifeguard.

Instead, I concentrate on crossing the pathway to the final single-storey building, which looks like it was built more recently than everything else, with more glass and fewer bricks than anything we've seen.

"State of the art, they say," continues Grandma. Who says, exactly, and what do they know about it?

To Autumn

A large mirror-ball dangles from the centre of the ceiling over buffed parquet that marks out the dancefloor in front of a box stage. The edge of the room is full of round-table booths with navy faux-velvet-covered seatbacks. We walk across a dark thick carpet that looks like it was designed to hide the horrors of what happens in this room, which smells gross, of stale smoke and old people. Dingy, is the only word for it, and Mum's voice repeats it in my head.

"This is the centrepiece of the whole park," says Grandma proudly. "We have bingo, quiz nights, fancy dress competitions, ballroom dancing displays, and guest bands. Wonderful." If you are over sixty maybe. "We'll pop up most evenings after dinner."

"Cool," I say, trying to mask my disappointment. I daren't look at Anne's face. No TV and now our evenings bookmarked for the kind of entertainment only ever enjoyed by people over the age of thirty.

We go back outside, and the contrast of natural light makes my eyes water. We start back towards the caravan, inevitably past the swimming pool. I hear the lifeguard calling orders again, but the fence blocks my view of her.

"I think we'll be okay going for a swim," I say, putting on my most grown up voice. "I can take care of Anne, they have lifeguards. We'll be fine!"

"We'll see."

Translation: "No chance."

Grandma puts forward a peace offering, "I'll show you the beach tomorrow, that always seems like a fun place for the other families."

To Autumn

CHAPTER THREE

As we're on our way back to the caravan my stomach starts to rumble – not finishing those sandwiches is coming back to haunt me, and the soggy Weetabix I had at six thirty this morning seems like days ago. All around us, families scoop up their kids and towels and make their way towards their own homes. They remind me of previous family holidays that feel much more preferable to the thought of going back to Grandma's right now. The past has a way of doing that, although, after what's happened this year, maybe it wasn't all as perfect as it seemed.

"Tonight is the super Saturday cabaret show at the clubhouse this evening," Grandma says, "my favourite night."

"Can't wait," I mutter, deflating like a spent balloon. We've been to those types of nights before, on holidays with Mum and Dad. The type of night where the performers wear red or blue blazers, and flirt with the old ladies for big tips, which Mum finds hilarious to watch. The nights tend to roll into one tedious show of pantomime-style singing and dancing to cheesy pop songs. They aren't usually aimed at teenagers, and I couldn't tell who actually enjoys those shows.

Anne was usually forced to join the holiday kids club where they have children's television presenter rejects acting like clowns trying to make bored small children laugh by pretending to fall over. The last few years we've gone camping in France, and I've been allowed to go out with the other "young adults". This means hanging out in large groups at the arcades or in someone's chalet, trying to avoid the eyes of security guards. I hope I can persuade Grandma that's what I should be doing here as well.

Just around the corner from the shower block, we pass a phone box and I make a mental note of the location. At least Dad remembered to give me a pile of twenty pence coins, for us to phone home whenever we want.

The concrete in my stomach expands while I'm thinking about Dad and home, so I switch my brain to nicer thoughts: eating chocolate, Take That's *Everything Changes* album, laughing with Michelle and Tanith, the lifeguard from the pool. The lifeguard? Where did she come from? Looking like something out of *Baywatch*. An image of her in the red swimsuit running down a beach like Pamela Anderson won't leave my head no matter what else I try to think of.

We arrive back at Grandma's home, and I listen attentively to what she is saying, blocking out those thoughts.

"Fish fingers, chips, and peas for dinner?" she asks and at last we have some common ground. "Your dad told me that's a favourite for both of you."

"Perfect," I say. Even Anne manages a smile. "Can we call Dad later? He'll be home from the hospital after six."

"Yes, good idea, I'll call him and let him know you arrived safe and sound when we're on the way to the club house. Why don't you two go and have a wash in the shower block while I start dinner?"

Seizing the opportunity to have a break from Grandma and possibly even a moment fully to myself, I say, "Yes!" a little louder than needed. "Come on, Anne, let's grab our stuff."

†

We walk towards the shower block, and I start to enjoy the break from endless small talk and false smiles. I'm trying to remember the route we took earlier, but it seems impossible when every row of caravans we pass looks the same as the one before it. My instinct says if we keep heading in one direction we'll come to the centre of the park, or the edge of the park, or somewhere we recognise.

I've no idea what to say to Anne. Her quiet calm about everything makes me nervous. She's too hard to read, along with her refusal to talk. The opposite of me.

We pass one final row and suddenly we meet brick walls rather than flimsy yellow. Following the uneven path around the block, we find a door that has a stick figure wearing a black triangle. Mum says this is a woman wearing a cape, not a dress, or perhaps a woman towelling herself off after a bath. Inside are a small number of individual cubicles, each with their own brightly coloured PVC curtain. No doors. The floor is covered in water and floating grass. I've never been more thankful for flip flops.

"Are you okay to shower by yourself?" I ask Anne. She nods confidently, takes a towel and her washbag from me, heads into a cubicle and pulls the curtain sharply across the rail.

"Here's your soap." I pass a fluorescent blue travel soap dish inside the curtain. She grabs it from my hand without a word. I stand for a moment, looking at Anne's cubicle, wishing I could be like her. What a relief it must be, not having to talk to anyone.

At least at Anne's age no one expects her to react to what's happened with Mum in any specific way. No one is asking her to be mature and brave about it all. I had to promise Dad I would be grown up and take care of Anne and not be a nuisance for Grandma while we are here, just because I am older.

I take the cubicle two down from Anne, to give her some space. I turn the shower on quickly, just in time to cover the sound of my tears as I let go and cry into the lukewarm water.

When Anne was very little, Mum used to dress us in matching outfits and Anne was like my second shadow. I thought coming away together could be a chance for us to remember that at one time in our lives, we were friends.

I want Anne to know that I'm just as scared and confused as she is, and that this situation isn't an easy one to understand or be in. Being sent away for the whole summer and leaving everything we know behind sucks big time. It feels like we might never go home and even if we do, can it ever be the same again? What if Mum doesn't get better? I long to return to those times before the car crash, and wish I'd appreciated how easy things were. I really wish I'd never kissed Beth.

I dance around to try and make sure my whole body gets a bit of a freshen up, and after a few seconds the water warms up and the pressure increases. The water feels comforting as it washes away the tears and runs through my blonde curls and down my body. I'm not yet used to the curves and hips that replace the matchstick frame I had before my period started a few years ago. I knew where I was with that body. Now, every time I dare to look at myself, there's something new to discover and understand.

I miss having someone to talk to about these things, and there isn't some all-knowing place we can access to find out answers to questions about growing up and puberty. There's no way I could ask anyone at school without being totally humiliated. The way they all talk about bodies and sex, even Michelle and Tanith, makes me feel like I know nothing at all. Where do they find these things out?

    I close my eyes and enjoy the last few moments of peace, before stepping out of the safety of the water and into the humid drying space in the cubicle. I dress as quickly as I can back into my jeans, T-shirt and flip-flops, trying not to make the clothes wet from the floor. I wrap the towel around my hair, hoping it will be okay to walk back to the mobile home like this as I've left my detangling comb and hair mousse in the tiny bedroom. Anne's waiting for me when I pull back the curtain.

†

    As soon as Grandma catches sight of me, she gasps and pulls me into the home. "You can't walk around like that!"

    "But my hair is wet!"

    "That's what hair dryers are for. Why didn't you take one with you?"

    "Don't have one."

    "But you can't possibly go out with wet hair. You'll catch your death."

    "Mum lets me dry it naturally. If I use a hair dryer it makes the curls massive and frizzy. And hair dryers are bad for hair. They damage the follicles."

"Your mother always did have some funny ideas." The words hit me like a slap on the cheek.

"My mum knows what is best for me," I say, trying not to let my voice waiver.

Grandma pauses and composes herself. "I'm sure she tried her best," she manages, as a kind of peace offering.

I swivel round and continue to the bedroom, Anne following behind me. She looks at me, puts her toiletries and towel away tidily, and sits on her bunk while I fix my hair. There's a small mirror on the back of the door. I rub my hair more roughly than usual with the towel, and then with the comb, try and fight a way through the already formed curls, desperate to stop any tangles. Finally, I pile on the mousse, hoping it will do its magic trick of matting down the frizz. I hate my curls.

"Dinner's ready," Grandma says in a friendlier voice than just before.

I open the door and sit down with Anne in the dining booth.

"Robyn, dear, would you mind setting the table for us?"

"Course not." Grandma points to the cutlery drawer and I open it and grab everything we need, carefully laying three places, rather than my normal trick of dumping the knives, forks and napkins in the middle of the table and telling everyone to help themselves.

Grandma brings over two plates and the concrete in my stomach hardens. She has served fish fingers, crinkle cut oven chips, and peas. Real peas, not mushy peas. Anne only eats mushy peas. She's always been a fussy eater. I thought, as Grandma said she had spoken to Dad, she'd have been told this.

Anne pushes the peas around her plate.

"Umm, Anne doesn't like peas like that, she only eats the mushy ones from a can."

"That's no excuse, it's all the same food!" Grandma booms. "You'll sit there, young lady, and eat every last mouthful on that plate. Or no dessert and no club house." Anne puts down her knife and fork.

"I can sit here all night, if that's what it takes. I know your dad's had to let things slide at home lately, but we'll have none of that when you're with me. Understand? You will both do as you're told."

I don't know why I'm being tarred with Anne's brush, I'm perfectly happy to eat real peas, I like them better than the tinned mushy sludge we have at home. I work quickly to clear my plate.

"Why don't you try them with ketchup?" Anne dips her fishfinger into the puddle of ketchup but gives the peas a wide berth.

"Well, Robyn, you may have some ice cream for dessert," Grandma says, pitting me against Anne.

"No, that's alright, thanks, I'm full." In response, Anne finishes the fish fingers. Grandma is watching her with a close eye. Finally, when there's only one chip and a large handful of peas left, Grandma relents and tells Anne she only

To Autumn

has to eat one pea. Anne sizes up the plate and picks the smallest looking green ball, spears it with her fork and chews it with a pained look on her face. She takes a huge gulp of water and makes a big show of washing it down.

I slump back in my seat able to relax at last.

"Clear the table will you, Robyn? Now, if you put all the dirty dishes into the washing up bowl, you can take that down to the central block and wash the dishes there. Much easier in that big sink. The washing up liquid and rubber gloves are just under the sink here." Before I have a chance to feel annoyed, I grab everything and leave. At least it'll give me a few more minutes to myself.

I end up taking a different route from before, I have no idea how, but it means I pass the phone box, which has a short queue of kids at various ages paired with fraught looking fathers.

†

I'm making hard work of the washing up, trying to go as slowly as possible. Anything to not have to go back to the caravan too soon. I'm joined by plenty of other kids who've also drawn the short straw as chief dish washer. I'm jealous of their marigolds.

A couple of the boys are more interested in throwing soap suds back and forth than washing up, and my clothes suffer the consequences. I don't feel brave enough to join in yet. A father walks by on his way to the shower block, and more orderly washing up resumes, followed by whispers and giggles, and fart noises.

A few of the kids start talking about having to go to the clubhouse tonight, clearly under duress like me, and there are hasty discussions about how they can argue to be allowed to escape the torture.

One of the older boys, about my age, makes eye contact. He's nearly finished his bowl of washing up, having sped through the plates like a demon.

"Hey," he says. He looks a bit like Mario Lopez, all rich ochre and dimples, but thankfully no mullet. If Michelle and Tanith were here, they'd be all over him. They're mad about Zach and Slater from *Saved by the Bell*. I've always been more interested in what Jessie Spano's up to. "If you wash all the plates first and rinse them all together after, it won't take as long."

"Thanks," I say, "we use the dishwasher at home, so I've not really done loads of washing up before."

"Where you from?"

"Wimbledon. London. We're staying with our gran for the summer. First time."

"Cool. I've always wanted to go to London. We live in Coventry, which is boring. But we come here every single summer."

"Is it as bad as it seems?" I ask, hoping to find the secret to making the summer better.

"Depends… sometimes cool people stay."

"I hope I find them. They're not gonna be in the club house, are they? Gran's making us go there tonight."

"You never know. Maybe we'll see you there, later?" he asks.

"Definitely. I don't think my sister and I have a choice."

"It's not that bad. Sort of. Well not if you can escape the 'rents. How old's your sister? My brother's ten. And annoying. But the 'rents only let me out if I take him with me."

"Anne's nine. She's not that annoying. But she doesn't speak."

"What, like she can't speak?"

"No, she's just stopped talking for a while. Apparently, the specialist doctor said there's nothing to worry about, like she'll speak again, but when she wants to. So, Dad was like, just let her be and don't make a big deal about it."

"Okay...well, I should go back, or they'll send out a search party. See ya. Maybe meeting other kids'll help your sister. I'm Dean by the way. My brother's called Jamie." He holds out his hand to shake. I've only ever shaken hands with grownups before.

"Robyn. Anne's my sister. My grandma's Gloria. Mrs Gale. She comes here every summer too." He loads his washing up bowl and heads off. Too soon, I am heading back to the caravan.

†

"Lovely, Robyn, nice and clean. That wasn't too bad, was it?" Grandma asks, inspecting the dishes the second I walk through the door.

"No, it was okay, and I talked to some of the other kids down there."

"Wonderful. You'll both be making friends in no time. That's the beauty of a holiday home in a place like this, there's always lots of nice people around. I'll introduce you to some of my friends later tonight. Right, let's be on our way, shall we? I don't want to lose my favourite booth. It has the best view of the stage!"

"Remember we said we could call Dad on the way?" I ask. "I can bring the coins Dad gave us."

"Yes. I will, dear. Don't be silly, I'll pay." We head back out again. Time feels like it will be measured through the perpetual entry and exit of the caravan.

As we stroll towards the payphone, I start to see little differences between each of the homes. Colourful curtains adorn some, windchimes others. Maybe it's not such a maze after all.

The queue for the phone box is shorter than it was earlier, and we wait patiently as a son and dad combo finish a tearful goodbye into the handset. Grandma takes out a silver coin and her red pocketbook to look for the phone number.

"I know the number!"

"That's alright, love. I'll just look it up in my book and then we'll know we've got it right, won't we? I don't want to waste ten pence speaking to a stranger." She picks up the phone to dial. My fingers itch in anticipation of taking the handset. I know that a measly ten pence won't last very long on the call.

"Hello… John? Yes, it's Mum," Grandma says, and I can almost hear the ticking of a stopwatch quickly winding down against the ten pence's worth of time. "Yes, they're here, no problems at all, and we've had a lovely afternoon looking round the holiday park and having fish fingers for tea... No, they are no bother at all. You know I am happy to have them here to help you out. That's my job as your mother… Okay, I'll tell them, yes… hang on, I'll hand you over."

Grandma passes me the black telephone receiver, and I grab it eagerly. I place it to my ear, but all I can hear are the mechanical pips signalling that the money's run out. I put the phone back in the cradle, determined not to let any tears spill out. Anne takes my hand.

"Your father said to tell you both he loves you very much and hopes we have a lovely time."

"We wanted to speak to him ourselves."

"Maybe next time my dear. We should head on to the clubhouse, or we'll miss the beginning of the show."

†

Inside the club house, Grandma makes a beeline for the booth that is closest to the stage. Although the seats are practically on top of the sound system, we do have a cracking view of centre stage.

Grandma turns to me. "Here's five pounds. Why don't you go and buy us some drinks? I'll have a ginger ale." She's not really asking.

"Okay, Grandma. Anne do you wanna come with me?" Anne shrugs but stands up. As we walk over to the bar, I catch sight of Dean and a younger version of Dean who I guess is Jamie. They join us in the queue.

"Hi!"

"Hi! This is Anne," I say, shoving her towards the boys in a kind of whole-body handshake. "I met Dean at the washing up sinks. And this must be Jamie?"

"James!" the younger boy corrects me.

"Sorry," Dean jumps in, "he's trying to be more manly this summer."

"Right." I order our drinks and look over at Grandma who is waving at us to hurry up. "Well, maybe see you on the dancefloor later? Do kids dance here?" What am I talking about?

"Yes, they do… and maybe if you're there, we'll join you," Dean says, his cheeks going pink.

"You're on," I respond, glad to be making some friends who seem normal. Anne picks up her coke, and I take my lime and soda and Grandma's ginger ale to the table.

†

To Autumn

"Who was that you were talking to?" Grandma asks as soon as we return, not even a "thank you" first.

"Just some kids I met when I did the washing up. The ones I told you about."

"I see. I didn't realise you meant boys. I'd better introduce myself to their parents and make sure they are suitable friends for you both."

"They're really nice! Dean showed me a better way to do the washing up."

"Did he?"

A drum roll starts from the stage.

"Well shush now, and we'll talk about this later. The show is starting." A man, in what Mum and Dad call a penguin suit, walks onto the stage towards the spotlight. Grandma waves at him and in return he gives her a little wink. The concrete lump in my stomach does heavy somersaults. Everyone in the room is watching us.

"That's my gentleman friend, Mr Hooper," Grandma whispers. Oh my days. Blood is pounding loudly in my ear, and I can hardly hear what he says to the audience, but soon enough everyone is laughing, so it must've been amusing. Then the band strikes up – all equally grey haired and round – a drummer, a keyboardist and guitarist, dressed in matching shiny red jackets.

"Good evening, ladies and germs." Cue polite laughter from the audience members who are mostly around Grandma's age. "First of all, we have a special treat tonight. I'd like to introduce you to our first performer. Making her debut on this stage and sharing with us a few famous tunes from her homeland of Australia, please give a warm welcome to Miss Autumn Mitchell," Mr Hooper says into the microphone, before, thankfully, stepping to the side. And then she walks onto the stage and the breath sails out of me. The lifeguard. She's going to sing to me.

To Autumn

CHAPTER FOUR

She steps forward, front and centre, and the spotlight lands right on her. She's wearing a glittery silver dress over leggings, and her hair has been teased with hairspray and backcombed to within an inch of its life. Her makeup is just right though, and she fits in perfectly with the setting, even if she's wearing a very different look from the sporty *Baywatch* figure I saw earlier. She stands fearlessly, looking perfectly at home on the stage, with the confidence of having done this many times before. Maybe she has, just not here at this holiday park. She adjusts her dress and looks to the band to start. Immediately they kick off with a melody I recognise. There's nothing like a bit of Kylie to win the crowd over; everyone loves the princess of pop.

"There's nothing like a bit of Kylie, is there?" Autumn asks, and not waiting for a reply, breaks into the opening lines of "I Should Be So Lucky". I hold my breath as she begins, and it feels like rainbows are dancing inside me. There's just her singing to me; everyone else disappears like at the pool, and with every ounce of me I want to make her so lucky in love. The sudden interlude of roaring applause and whistles break me out of a daze, and I let out a long breath. My chest is hammering and I'm sure that everyone else can see a big flashing neon sign above my head, calling out my reaction.

"Thank you. You gotta love the princess of pop, right?" she asks, smiling at the audience's response to her. "Although, between us, she'll always be Charlene to me." Was that a *Neighbours* reference? "I'm only allowed two numbers tonight. How about a bit of INXS?" The audience quiets, not sure what they're about to hear. She's taking a bit of gamble given most of this crowd are much closer to Grandma's age than mine. But then, with just her voice and the keyboard accompanying, Autumn starts an acoustic version of "Beautiful Girl" that is raw and beautifully different from the version I know. No one cares that we're listening to a weird indie rock song. At the end, everyone stands up, including Grandma, and I join in. Autumn smiles and bows awkwardly, then steps off into the make-shift wings.

"Well," Mr Hooper says as he clambers back up the shoddy staircase attached to stage left, "looks like it's a

To Autumn

triumph from Down Under. Thank you, Autumn, thank you, audience. Autumn, we hope to see you back on the stage this time next week, don't we, ladies and gentlemen?" The crowd claps again but Autumn is long gone into the mysterious closed off world backstage. Autumn, Autumn. Her name bounces in my ears in time to the applause.

When we sit down, Grandma looks at me and says, "Well, she seems to have caught your attention, Robyn!" My cheeks betray me before I can respond.

"Can we have another drink please, Grandma?" is the best I can muster in a weak distraction tactic.

"Yes, but you'll have to go yourself. Mr Hooper usually does a number next, before the magician comes on stage. I can't miss that."

†

There's a long queue at the serving area. I'm humming the INXS song, and picturing Autumn up on stage singing, this time with only me in the audience. Just as she's about to bring me up on stage to join her, to sing to me whilst looking deep into my eyes, Mr Hooper's in-real-life voice fills the room, drowning my daydream.

Dean and Jamie come over to me at the bar.

"We're gonna go to the playground now," Dean says. "Wanna join?"

I'd rather stay here in this claustrophobic sweat box and find a way to introduce myself to Autumn.

"Okay," I say, and Dean smiles. "I'll need to check with Grandma first. What about Anne?"

"If she wants. There'll be a few others there."

"Let's go and talk to Grandma when I take over her ginger ale then," I say.

†

Dean carries the drink, having swiped it from the countertop while I was still handing over the ninety pence. He hands it to Grandma, but she doesn't let us talk until Mr Hooper finishes a song that sounds like it belongs in a black and white film.

"That's one of my favourites," she says. "He sings it very well."

"My parents said that, too, Mrs Gale." Dean offers his hand to Grandma. "I'm Dean Jackson. This is my brother, James. We met Robyn at the sinks earlier."

"Dean was the boy who showed me how to wash up better," I say.

"Yes, my parents are resident mobile homeowners, too. We've been coming here for five years." Dean sounds like he has done this before. "Anyway, James and I were wondering if Robyn, oh and Anne of course, would be able to join us and some of the other kids, in the playground?"

Grandma looks Dean up and down, then, finally, says, "Alright. But only until it gets dark. Then I want you right back here. And take your coats." I'm surprised how readily she agrees and relish the thought of some time to spend away from her direct supervision, even if it means I won't be able to find a way to become acquainted with Autumn tonight. I doubt the holiday park staff will be at the adventure playground.

    I pick up my coat and Anne slides around the table to join us. As she's wriggling out, Mr Hooper walks in our direction. Grandma puts her hand on Anne's shoulder indicating we should wait. Dean's already across the room, well on the way to freedom.

    "Girls, this is my friend, Mr Hooper. Say hello!"

    "Hi."

    "You can do better than that."

    "Hello, Mr Hooper. I enjoyed your song."

    "Thank you, dear. You must be Robyn," Mr Hooper says, in his west country accent. "Which means the little one must be Anne." My cheeks hurt from forcing the biggest smile I can rally.

    "Wasn't that Australian girl just fantastic? Did you like her Robyn? Are you a big Kylie fan?"

    "Who isn't?" I say, feeling the blood rush to my cheeks again.

    "I think Robyn has a little crush." Gran laughs and Mr Hooper lets out a bellowing guffaw.

    "I do not. I just like Kylie a lot, like Mr Hooper said. Can we go now?"

    Grandma hesitates before finally saying yes. "But back before it's dark." She can't help to remind us. Still, the prospect of being allowed time without adults is too significant to argue over the curfew.

I steer Anne towards the exit and as we pass the bar, an Australian accent hits my ears and almost stops me in my tracks, causing Anne to stumble into me. I look over to see Autumn surrounded by a group of guys and girls about her age. I keep moving towards the door but take a little glance backwards before we exit. One of the older guys places his hand on Autumn's lower back.

Dean and Jamie appear, blocking my view of Autumn, and I remember that we're meant to be following them outside to the playground. The sun is already making her final descent, meaning we don't have long before we turn into Cinderella.

"We're coming," I say, and we follow them out.

†

Outside, the evening is cool, and the sea air breezes over the dunes, creating goose bumps on my arms. I'm glad I have my jacket. We arrive at the adventure playground, which is mostly monkey bars, wobbly walking benches made from splintered wood, and climbing frames stuck in damp bark. There are a few other kids around, mostly other teens also escaping their parents. Anne walks over to one of the swings and within a few seconds is lurching to and fro, pushing the frame to its limits. When we were younger, we used to try to make the swing go right over the top bar. We'd heard someone had once done it and lived to tell the tale.

Jamie takes the swing next to her and follows her lead. They seem happy in a mute enjoyment of the steady loops back and forth.

    Dean pulls me towards where the older kids are standing in a disjointed cluster, passing round a can of cider. The group is an eclectic mix of boys and girls, two I recognise from washing up. The youngest boy, who looks about fourteen, is smoking. There's a thick combination of hormones and desire sitting like a fog around us. Or maybe that's just the smoke from the cigarette.

    Our voices hold a secret whisper as we all introduce ourselves, although I instantly forget everyone's name. Dean drinks a sip from the can when it comes to his turn and then hands it to me. Mum and Dad let me have wine on special occasions and last Christmas Mum even bought me some alcoholic lemonade to try. I take a big swig, imagining Grandma's horror if she were to catch me in the act, and hand it on to the next person. I make a face as I swallow it. Warm cider from a can does not taste as nice as white wine from the fridge, or even five percent hard lemonade. Dean laughs.

    "Oi!" I say, and he stands a little closer. "We don't have much time, it'll be dark soon," I say, to change the focus away from my lack of appreciation of warm, flat cider.

    "That's ages away," Dean responds, dismissive of my urgency.

    "So, what else happens here?"

"This place isn't that bad, you know. The pool is pretty good, at least it has a slide, and they have a load of inflatables, and do water games. And in the club house, there's the rec room with a TV, some games, pool, table tennis, and some arcade machines."

"Okay. My Grandma didn't show us that bit."

"How come you haven't been here before?"

"I think we might have done when I was younger, that's what Dad said, but I don't remember any of it. And we don't usually see Grandma that often. We never have really, at least not since Anne was born."

"Are your parents coming to stay as well?"

"No, they're out of the country. Dad had to work abroad, and Mum went with him, so…"

Dean touches my wrist then pulls me away from the group. "I want to show you something," he says, and one of the boys whistles as we move away. Anne and Jamie are still swinging, and I follow Dean, wondering what can be so amazing that he has to show me right now.

At the far end of the playground, there's some overgrown trees and long grass, and next to that a faded sign that says "Nature Reserve." We go into the mess of branches and leaves, following a well-trodden, bark-chip pathway. A few steps in and there's an empty pond and a little bench. Dean holds an arm out gesturing I should sit down. This is what he was excited to show me?

To Autumn

We sit down, and Dean edges close enough that I all can smell is Lynx Africa. "So, are you missing your friends? Boyfriend?"

"I don't have a boyfriend," spills out before I have time to think.

"Oh really? Me neither. I mean, my girlfriend dumped me right before exams started. But now I think it was probably for the best. Hopefully I haven't failed all of my GCSEs because of her. Have you ever had a…?"

"Oh loads. My best friends, Michelle and Tanith and me, we've had loads of boyfriends. But I don't have one right now. So, if I have failed all my GCSEs, it won't be the fault of my non-existent boyfriend." My mouth is saying things ahead of my brain. I'm playing catch up to my own words.

"Cool," Dean says, and leans back and stretches his arm out, resting it on the back of the bench just behind me.

"Grandma said she wanted us back before dark," I say. I stand up, hopefully not too abruptly, and jog back through the mess of green, towards Anne. Anne's still swinging away, and Jamie's now standing to the side watching her, and talking to her, even though he's not getting any replies.

"Time to go, Sis," I say, and Anne does one more swing then jumps off, landing steadily on her feet. Dean comes trailing out of the nature reserve, and heads straight towards the boys drinking cider.

"Bye!" I say, waving at the back of Dean's head. I walk as fast as I can back to the club house, Anne trotting alongside me to keep up.

To Autumn

CHAPTER FIVE

The night is very dark and I'm sitting on the bench in the nature reserve. I can't see much, but I can hear birds flutter against the moonlight in the trees behind me. I can feel the warmth of someone next to me, keeping the chill in the air at bay. My eyes start to adjust to the lack of light and come to the silhouette of a person. They feel safe. I lean back into the bench. The person puts their arm behind me on the bench then lets it drop onto my neck. I put my head onto their shoulder and my ear grazes soft hair. A floral scent wafts around us. I lift my head up with a smile and realise I'm sitting next to Autumn.

I wake with a gasp. I sit up and bang my head on something hard above me. Where am I? There's light from a streetlamp coming in through the gaps between the blinds. Within a few seconds I can see the edge of the bunk bed, then the mirror on the door, and I remember that I'm in a caravan, Gran's caravan.

My pyjamas are damp with sweat despite the coolness of the night. I can hear the deep sleep of Anne's breathing, and the dread in my chest starts to fade. I turn my pillow over to the cool side that isn't soaked in sweat and lie back down.

I practise a trick Mum showed me when I had nightmares after our dog was run over. She told me to focus hard on my breathing, to count the breath in for five and out for five, then to look around and list what I can see, then hear, then smell and finally touch. I do this now, repeating it three times until I start to feel sleepy again. Just as my eyes are closing, I fall back into the dream, sitting next to Autumn on the bench. A familiar mix of delight, excitement, and fear battle against each other in my stomach.

"Oh no, not this again," I whisper, making Anne stir. I freeze and wait for her breathing to return to the long slow breaths of sleep. I hear a voice that sounds a lot like mine saying, "Find a boyfriend. For Mum's sake." The words repeat incessantly around my head. I try again with Mum's breathing trick, and after a long while I nod off.

†

To Autumn

"Wakey-wakey, rise and shine!" Grandma's shrill call rattles through the rickety partition walls and the bunkbed frame. I sit up and bang my head again.

"Fu-", I manage to stop myself before finishing a word that will most definitely put me in trouble if Anne or Gran hears it. I rub my head instead, whilst I disentangle my legs from the blankets. As Anne climbs down from the top bunk, I drum up my nerve and spirit to face a cheery-sounding Grandma. Thankfully there's been no more strange dreams.

Anne opens the bedroom door to a view of Grandma, fully dressed in sportswear. Not the sort of sportswear a professional athlete would wear, closer to a Mad Lizzie workout from eighties breakfast television. The ensemble is pristine and matching though, and the flannel sweatband accessorises it perfectly.

"As today is your first morning, and a Sunday, I'll make bacon sandwiches for you when I return from my power walk with Mr Hooper," Grandma says, while she puffs trying to tie up her shoelaces. "This is a special treat, mind you, not what we have every day." Puff. "Robyn, be a dear and take the bacon out of the fridge and put the bread in the toaster, please. You could start the kettle boiling, too. I won't be long!" Grandma heaves herself out of the caravan and the door slams shut with the gust of her departure.

I have no idea what "long" means for Grandma, but I take the chance to have a good nose around the living area of the mobile home. I saw some funny things when I was looking for a TV yesterday. I open and shut each door quickly, in case Grandma returns. Anne's watching me wide-eyed, looking on in static encouragement. I know I'm not going to find a TV hidden away, but I do want a chance to find out more about Gran. She acts like we should know all about her already, but Dad never says much about her at home.

    I open the first cupboard and am almost hit on the head by a falling teacup. The cupboard is crammed full of Royal memorabilia, plates and mugs mostly, including many specifically from Charles and Diana's wedding. Grandma wanted me to be called Diana because I happened to be born on their wedding day. Mum wasn't having any of it, according to Dad. She didn't want me burdened with a name that would always make people think of someone else. As these plates aren't what we ate from yesterday, I guess they probably aren't used for everyday eating, so I won't set the table with them. How funny to fill what little storage space there is with plates that aren't used.

    My mouth is dry, not surprising as I haven't had anything to drink since the sip of cider last night. I open the fridge to see what Grandma has. There's orange juice, which I pour out for me and Anne into miniature glasses that I find in yet another cupboard stacked full of toy-sized crockery. Everything's smaller than normal. Anne gulps hers down almost all in one. I fill the kettle, which is only big enough to make two cups of tea at a time, and switch it on. I take the fresh pack of bacon out of the fridge, as Grandma asked.

To Autumn

    I carry on exploring. In a drawer next to the sink, I find some foil. Then I open the oven to see if there is a grill pan, which there is, a tiny one. I layer the foil on it, then squeeze on six pieces of bacon. I find a sliced loaf of bread in the one-and-only tall cupboard, next to the fridge, and take out enough slices for a sandwich each. Of course, only two slices can fit in the toaster at a time. I load the first round. Anne prefers untoasted bread for her bacon sandwiches anyway. I find three plates and give them to Anne to lay on the table. The kettle boils, and I dig around for tea bags and cups and pour out two cups of tea to brew. I add a milk bottle, brown sauce, and ketchup from the fridge to Anne's preparation of the table.

    Less than ten minutes after she left, Grandma returns. "I just love to start the day with exercise, keeps me looking young and hip." Grandma has not broken a sweat, but she has picked up a copy of the *Mail on Sunday*. "Robyn, could you just stick that bacon under the grill for me? Turn the knob to the right. And I have milk and sugar in my tea. Good girl." Grandma sweeps into her bedroom at the other end of the kitchen galley. I follow her instructions. The saliva inducing smell of bacon cooking soon fills the caravan, and my stomach rumbles loudly.

    I can hear Grandma banging about in her room, and just as the toast pops, I remember the tea which has now been stewing for a long time. I hope Grandma likes builders' tea. I swap over the bread in the toaster, drain the tea bags out of the cups, add milk to both, sugar to one and place them on the table. I check on the bacon in the oven and try to turn it using a fork, which is hard when the slices keep slipping about on the greasy foil. I leave the two that won't turn over, but the smell tells me they are cooking just right. Anne empties her glass of OJ, and I refill it for her. I take three sheets of kitchen towel from the roll and ask Anne to put them next to each place. As the second batch of toast pops up, I plate the six slices of bread and then open the oven door and pull out the bacon. Just as I place the final sandwich together, Grandma steps out of her bedroom.

"Make sure you turn the grill off, Robyn, we don't want a fire, do we?" is all Grandma says as she walks past me and sits into the booth and squirts brown sauce on her sandwich. I sit down next to her and add ketchup to my sandwich. "I didn't know you were so handy, Robyn. You can help me with all sorts of things."

I munch the now-cold sandwich. "I started making them for us when Mum first became too ill to cook, just to help carry on our weekend tradition." After months of making them, I have perfected the crispiness and the timing against the kettle and toaster, ensuring both the tea and sarnies can be served hot. Well, I would have done if the toaster had more than two slots. Bacon sarnies were one of the few things Mum still enjoyed eating, right up until the day she went into hospital.

"I'm glad your father carried on my tradition of a Sunday bacon sandwich," Grandma says.

To Autumn

†

We're dressed in our swimmers, shorts, and sunhats, and lathered in Factor 30. Under the weight of three towels, a bucket and spade for Anne, a book for me, and a picnic lunch in Grandma's asbestos-lined cool box, the three of us stumble out of Grandma's and head towards the beach, following quite a few other families.

The holiday park has direct access, and the path runs past the playground where I was with Dean and the others last night. There are some empty cans of cider littering the roundabout.

Grandma tuts. "I hope that mess has nothing to do with you two and your new friends," she says. "There's always troublemakers in this playground at night. Perhaps you'd better stay away from here after dark."

"Whatever you want, Grandma," I say, and pick up the pace to avoid the magnetic pull of memories from sitting right there on the bench with Dean and dreaming about Autumn afterwards. I'm wading in treacle again as I can barely lift my legs up and down to keep going as fast as possible towards the salty sea air.

The dunes are a bit of a trek as the narrow, gorged paths are deep with loose sand. My feet sink and slip with each step, and I sweat to make progress clambering up with my hands full, despite the cool gusts of air coming over from the sea. Even when there's sun, it can't just be a nice, hot, clear day. Finally, I reach the top, with Anne and Grandma puffing behind me. I take in the view which feels strangely familiar, as though I have stood in this very spot before. The stretch of sand around the curve of the land, the yellow flags on bending poles marking the safe swim area, the collection of families setting up deck chairs in front of unsteady windbreakers: the sight of every British beach on a slightly warm summer day.

In the distance the lifeguard's whistle blows at a swimmer who's gone outside of the marked area. He's not wearing a Smugglers Cove uniform, which means Autumn won't be found lifeguarding the beach.

The sand becomes walkable where it's more densely packed under foot, and I turn left to find us a spot that seems the right distance away from the sea and other families, just as Mum would have done.

Jamie and his parents are a bit farther up the beach, but thankfully there's no sign of Dean with them. I don't want him to ask why I ran off right after he put his arm around me. I'm not even sure I could answer.

The deckchair attendant comes over and Grandma pays fifty pence to hire just one deckchair. "These young'uns can move themselves up and down easily, but with my knees I'd better have a chair," she says.

I'm sure this announcement is to cover for the real reason, that she doesn't want to part with the extra one pound. Not that it matters, only nanas sit in deck chairs, and I'd never be seen in one. Besides, there's no way you can catch an even suntan sitting in them, just red knees and a sore back.

To Autumn

    Anne and I lay down our towels, having to work together, as the towels flap unforgivingly in our faces, wafting sand all over the place. We finally lay them down, and Anne takes her bucket to start building a sandcastle. I make myself comfortable and find a position face down. Leaning on my elbows to read whilst giving the sun a direct path to do its tanning magic, I use Grandma as a shield from the breeze. This also helps me to not have to expose my body too much to the world; there's no chance of me prancing about in just a bikini, not caring what anyone thinks. I'm not one of those girls.
    I open my book, just as Grandma starts talking. Typical. She nags at us, "Make sure you've put enough sun cream on, both of you." Then confusingly, she transfers straight into, "Oh hello, dear. I thought you sang just wonderfully last night. Robyn here was a big fan, too."
    I feel the disadvantage of facing the sand, and struggle to twist my head round to see who Grandma's talking to. I'm met with a view of what is, unmistakably, a swimmer's body, dressed in a perfectly-fitting and flattering black halter-neck bikini – just the bikini and nothing else – outlined against the brightening sun. I overrule an impulse to remove the childish neon pink sunglasses I'm wearing. I attempt to style them out instead, along with the tankini and shorts Dad bought for me. Better than the worn-out almost-transparent green number I was forced to put up with last summer.

"Oh, thank you, Mrs…?" says that silky voice. Autumn.

"Mrs Gale. I'm a friend of Mr Hooper's," Grandma replies.

"Thank you, Mrs Gale. It was a lot of fun. I'm very grateful to Mr Hooper and the band for allowing me to perform." Autumn speaks in a tone I've heard often before, of young people in undesired conversations with annoying adults: just about polite. "I hope I can sing again soon," she continues with more sincerity. Yes, please.

Grandma gestures at me. "This is my eldest granddaughter, Robyn. Anne over there is the baby of the family." The blushing redness from last night returns to my cheeks, as I roll over to face Autumn and Grandma properly.

"Hi," we both say at the same time, only mine comes out as a squeak, sounding nothing like my real voice. There's a pause. I can't think of anything cool to say, and instead I'm recalling the warmth of her body and the excitement of her hair grazing my ear, from my dream. A tingle runs the length of me. Can I stop my body betraying me once more before everyone notices?

Just as the conversation gap is about to become awkward, Autumn says, "I think I saw you in the audience last night, too. The booth right at front? I'm glad I made a good impression. It was hard to tell how INXS would go down with that crowd. Kylie's a safer bet." Hang on, did she just say she noticed me last night?

"Even if you prefer Charlene?" I ask. Autumn gives me a wink.

"Is that Keats you're reading?" she continues. Her words buzz in my ears. She's probably just being polite with me too. Performers in interviews always say they can't even see the audience from the stage because of the bright lights pointed right at their faces.

"Robyn's a very bright girl," Grandma jumps in, saving me from having to make a clever sounding response, "always earning As on her school work, her father tells me."

Still my stomach folds in on itself. I wish I could be like Anne and just draw shapes in the sand, avoiding the spotlight. It would save me from making a total tit of myself.

"Keats. Yes." I try and find my words. "We did a few poems for GCSE English. I think he's on the college's A-Level syllabus too, so…" When I was revising for the exams, I had to learn the odes off by heart. He was right on with "Ode on a Grecian Urn." Staying locked in the moment before true happiness, before everything goes to shit, is way better than the inevitable pain joy brings.

"Getting yourself a head start, then? I'm studying English Literature at Exeter and I'm a big fan of the English Romantics. My parents read him to me when I was little, and he kind of stuck. They even named me after–"

"'To Autumn'" I say, keen to show I know my stuff. "Wow, that's one of my favourites. Cool." I think I pull it off.

"No, they named me after 'Ode on a Grecian Urn'," Autumn says. "Sorry. That's my Australian sense of humour getting the better of me. We're all brutally sarcastic."

"No, it was funny!"

"'I wandered lonely as a cloud'…" Grandma suddenly interrupts.

"I think that's Wordsworth, Mrs Gale," Autumn says, with only the tiniest hint of sarcasm this time. "Well, I'd better head back to my friends. We only have one day off a week, but they insist on us all hanging out together." Autumn turns to walk away, but over her shoulder shouts, "Watch out for the sun Robyn, looks like your face is already burning."

Is she taking the piss out of me?

"Told you," Grandma says.

†

Is it possible to be two things at once? Happy and terrified about meeting Autumn? Impressed and wanting to impress? She's a goddess and I'm a geek. She's nice to old ladies and a fan of Keats. No one else I know cares about poetry. Michelle and Tanith are always taking the piss about my Keats obsession.

I watch Autumn saunter back to her friends and then join their game of volleyball without giving a second thought to me. Why would she want to spend time with a kid? I mean, if she's a uni student, she's likely to be at least three years older than me and sixteen to nineteen seems like an infinite chasm.

To Autumn

Mum has always been my go-to person to share matters of the heart, and now there are too many reasons I can't tell her what's going on. The one person I want to talk to about these feelings is the one person I can't tell. Worse than that, I have to pretend that none of the curiosity about Autumn is happening. No one else can guess. I should steer clear of her and then I won't find myself in trouble again. Whenever I'm around her, I become a hot mess.

I focus back on reading the odes, sinking into my own drowsy hemlock of sun warmth and foamy waves crashing at the shoreline, flicking my tongue up and down trying to work out if I could crush a grape with it. I can see those bold lovers on the famous urn, just before they kiss as if they are right in front of me. But then I turn the page and there sits "To Autumn" and suddenly the shape of the lovers looks a lot like Autumn and me.

I look over to Anne. Her castle is coming on, and she seems happy filling her bucket, patting it with a spade and carefully tipping out each load to add to the growing ramparts. After a while she's joined by Jamie, who brings reinforcements in the form of a set of buckets at various sizes and a few more spades.

Grandma has nodded off, snoring lightly under her straw hat. I rub in some more sun cream and pass the bottle to Anne, and then I feel the urge to submerge into the water. There are enough people splashing about in the waves; the water can't be that cold.

"I'm heading down to paddle," I say to Anne. "Don't move away from Grandma in case she wakes up." I sneak a look to our right where Autumn, her boyfriend, and the other Smugglers are involved in an epic touch rugby pile on. This means I am unlikely to catch anyone's attention.

I make my way to the shoreline, trying my hardest not to step on small children or large pebbles, which means weaving in and out a lot, before reaching the cool dense sand of the tideline.

I put a toe into the foam of a wave as it creeps up to my feet and it sends a shiver through my body. Okay, one toe at a time, then. Of course, I know that I should just run in and dive straight under, like I did when I was little and didn't care about seawater stinging my eyes or the pain of going through that moment of uncomfortable coldness. The thought of being swallowed up by the sea stops me, my body refuses to move. I inch forward and allow the next wave to wash over my left foot, then both feet.

When I reach ankle deep, I feel the hairs on my leg prickle, and I wish that I'd remembered to shave in the shower yesterday. Then I feel a hand on my shoulder. Without looking, I automatically know who it is from the mix of coconut sun cream and CK One scents. She has the softest of touches, and my knees are beginning to buckle. I just about hold it together.

"G'day, again. I saw you head in, and thought I'd join you. My mates are all too worried about ruining their hair to brave the water for a swim. Wusses. What's the point of coming to the beach if you don't go in the sea?" That voice…even when Autumn talks, she sings.

My feet sink into the seabed, like its quicksand, fixing me to the spot. Waves crash into me, but I stand firm. Part of me wishes the undercurrent would carry me off; part of me wants time to stand still.

"Your Gran's a riot, isn't she?" Autumn continues, oblivious to the effect she is having on me.

"You could say that…" I trail off, not wanting to disclose the words I would choose to describe her.

"She reminds me of my Nanna. Not ready to be old, and not afraid to speak her mind." A pretty accurate description. Maybe Autumn's made the measure of her after all. "A lot of the regulars here are like that," Autumn continues, "I get a sense it's a British thing. It was like that at the place I worked last summer, too."

"How long have you been in England?" I'm not sure where these words come from, but I'm thankful to have said something that is not completely embarrassing.

"About a year. I came over last summer before I started uni. I was a lifeguard at the local pool back home in Melbourne during high school, so it made sense to do something like that here, and better than going home during winter. Plus, they're happy to let me sing for you over here. I wasn't allowed to do that at the municipal, even though I tried. Those philistines said they didn't come along to hear someone wailing away, they only came to swim."

I smile in hope that it urges her to keep talking. I wonder if her boyfriend is going to join us. I try and find the nerve to ask, but she continues.

"You going in?" she asks. I hesitate, although my body is no longer telling me I'm torturing it. I've almost forgotten the water's cold. I'm just about to answer when she takes my hand and runs fast into the sea, pulling me with her.

She jumps as a wave crashes its way towards us, and we're both knocked off our feet, submerged into the salty water. Autumn smiles at me as we meet, face to face, right side up again. The shock of the cold passes quickly. Before I can change my mind, I dive back under. I'm enjoying letting go and the intimacy of being that close to her. When I resurface, though, Autumn is freestyling towards the buoy, leaving me treading water.

"No need to thank me!" she says, turning back quickly, before speeding off face down. I know I could keep up with her, but instead I watch her smooth gliding strokes carry her away.

CHAPTER SIX

The undercurrent swirls around me, making hard work of just bobbing up and down. The faces of other swimmers fly past me as though I'm watching a video loop on fast forward. I'm enjoying being a quiet part of the scene, not have to think about anything. The water keeps me afloat, and like osmosis, my anxiety pours through my skin and into the sea. The undercurrent can carry that away.

My stomach starts to grumble with hunger. I body surf towards the shoreline, hoping for lunchtime. On the shore, fathers are helping their kids make sandcastles, one dad is being buried in the sand by two identical boys who scream with laughter, and mothers are unpacking sandwiches. The summers of my childhood.

"I was just going to send Annie down to call for you. Ready for lunch?"

Grandma is unloading cheese and pickle rolls, real grated cheese not plastic slices, a tub of grapes and cartons of orange juice. There's a red wrapper in the cooler expressing a hint of KitKat. A proper picnic. I don't hold back, stuffing a roll straight in my mouth. I'm ravenous from the swim and the total loss of senses around Autumn. Anne gets stuck in straight away too.

"Don't eat too fast, girls, it'll give you indigestion. Didn't your mother teach you that?"

Does Grandma ever take those boxing gloves off? That constant criticism is unfair when Mum isn't here to defend herself. Mum's the one who comes down hardest about behaving. She was always nagging us to eat properly, eat our vegetables, do our laces up, brush our teeth. Now she's not there to do it, I miss even those bits about her.

I line up a retort, wanting to say that Mum, at least, isn't the kind who thinks her job is done by phoning once a week. But instead, when I open my mouth, a hiccup tumbles out. Anne stifles a laugh, and this catches me off guard enough that the hiccups stop almost immediately. This is the first time I've seen a real reaction from her since before Mum went into hospital. I take a breath, carry on eating, and ignore Grandma's smug I-told-you-so face.

"Save a roll for Mr Hooper, girls, he'll be stopping by to join us this afternoon."

To Autumn

After three token grapes, I unfold the KitKat (twos) and enjoy running my finger down the centre and snapping it open. I've always done it that way, ever since I saw it on a TV ad. I remember sitting on Mum's lap, and holding the chocolate bar in my hand, delighting in copying the red-nailed hand with precision, before we'd have a piece each. This afternoon, I give the second finger to Anne.

†

When we're finished, and after Gran has made me walk all the litter up to the overflowing bin, I settle back down on my towel. I cover my head with my T-shirt. I really don't want to have my face any redder, and I pick up the Keats. But I'm not in the mood for melancholy odes.

I put Keats away and take out the book I'd surreptitiously borrowed from the library back in Wimbledon. *Oranges Are Not the Only Fruit* was something I'd heard about one night when I was watching the author, Jeanette Winterson, being interviewed on TV, talking about being a gay writer. She said that the book was autobiographical even though she wrote it as a novel. Ever since then I'd wanted to read it, and I asked the camp librarian to order it in. It took months to arrive. I ordered it well before Mum caught me with Beth.

I didn't really think it was going to arrive, until it turned up a couple of weeks ago. I managed to read a few pages each night at home, but I was scared about being caught by Dad and him telling Mum, so I hadn't read beyond chapter two. When Dad said we'd be coming here, I thought I might have a chance to read it, so I made sure to pack the book inside my Keats. I'm banking on a guess that Anne and Grandma won't be aware of the story, and even if they are, I'll say I'm reading it for college.

    I steal one last look over to my right. Autumn is back in from her swim, shaking water over everyone. The girls scream. Her boyfriend and another guy tackle her, and between them, carry her towards the sea. I turn to the page bookmarked with my library card and settle in to find out what's next for Jeanette.

†

    "Robyn? Come on, love, time to pack up and go for a shower before dinner." I've just reached what I think is an important moment, where Jeanette meets a girl she likes called Melanie.

    "Just a sec," I mutter, not moving.

    "Robyn! You've had your head stuck in that book all afternoon. Come on, please." Why is everything always scheduled to adult-time, not Robyn-time? I slip my library card in to mark the page and look up. The beach is a lot quieter now. Even Anne has already put away her bucket and spade and is looking at me like I'm holding her up.

    "Good book is it?" says a man's voice, from behind Grandma.

To Autumn

"Mr Hooper. I didn't see you arrive. The book is okay. Just something for college."

"Come on, let's go, before the showers are too busy," says Grandma, and we heave off.

†

After dinner, I pack up the used dishes into the washing up bowl and start to leave for the sinks before I'm asked.

"Maybe you'd like to take Anne with you, as you said you had fun yesterday?" Grandma says.

"Sure. Anne, grab an extra tea towel, please." I pat my pocket and feel the twenty pence pieces I put in there earlier. I'm planning to make a call to Dad on the way back. He's always in on a Sunday night, him and Mum never miss *Heartbeat* or *Peak Practice*. He's kept up watching them since she's been in hospital, too, even though I know he secretly can't stand that "floppy-haired cockney wannabe" Nick Berry. He asked me to show him how to tape them for her to watch when she gets home. If she gets home.

Anne and I wash up at great speed – much easier with two of us – and in my head I plan my conversation with Dad. I don't want him to worry about us, even though we had no choice in being sent away. I run through the positives of being here: making some friends who are boys, sunny weather, fish fingers. I won't mention peas. Or Autumn.

As soon as we're done with the dishes, we walk over to the phone box. There's no queue today because everyone's having their dinner at this time. I hold the washing up bowl to my hip, pick up the phone, put in the coin and dial. Dad answers after barely one full ring.

"Dad!"

"Robyn?"

"Duh," slips out before I can help it.

"Sorry, I was expecting – I wasn't expecting you. How are you, my girls? Behaving?"

Why is the first thing parents want to know about always whether we're behaving properly?

I pull Anne in towards me and put the receiver between our heads. "As if we'd do anything else, Dad."

"Is Anne okay? You are looking after her, aren't you?"

"Dad! We've only been here a day and a half. Yes, I'm looking after her, and yes, she seems okay. She's here with me." I look at her. She smiles and does a thumbs up. "She says 'hello.'"

"How's Gran?" Is that all he wants to talk about?

"Grandma," I say with extra emphasis on the name she asked to be called, "is… trying."

"Good. I'm sure you'll all end up getting on like a house on fire." Where are all the dad jokes instead of odd clichés? "Have you made any friends yet?" he continues.

I don't understand why he sounds like we've never spoken to each other before. One of the only good things to come out of the whole situation had been becoming a bit closer to Dad, and knowing he is there for us. I hope that him sending us here doesn't undo all of that.

"Yeah, a couple of kids, one my age, one Anne's age." I don't mention Autumn. "How's Mum doing, did you see her today?"

"She's fine. Well, the same. No change. I'll make sure I keep her posted with all your news. You'll both have a brilliant summer holiday there, like I used to when I was your age. Gran and Aunty Di always spoiled me rotten."

"Thanks, Dad. Well, we better go back, I need to take the washing up back before Grandma wonders where we are."

"Of course. Well, girls, I love you both, I really do. As does your mum. She'll be pleased to hear you're doing well. Try and call me on Tuesday if you can, I want to wish you a happy birthday on the day."

"Love you, Dad," I say, before the pips put an end to our call. The queue has built up behind us, and we exit the booth as quickly as we can. Anne, as always, is unreadable. I wonder what is going on in that head of hers.

I can't let the thought out of my head that Dad sounded way weirder than normal. Not that we've ever had to speak on the phone to him that much before. We start to walk back to Grandma's, and I really hope she doesn't decide she needs to call Dad tonight, or we'll be busted for going behind both their backs.

Chapter Seven

For the first time in a long time, I wake up on a Monday morning and don't have to make a mad dash to leave for school on time. Not that I was very successful with that last term.

Long lazy lie ins are exactly what summer holidays are made for. I'd begun to dread turning up to school since we went on study leave for the GCSE exams. The concrete weighed in my stomach as a permanent feature during May and June. I can't even remember most of what happened during the exams. The personal, health, and social ed classes we had to go to after the exams are a blur. I vaguely remember being shown how to put a condom on a cucumber as all the girls giggled and whispered. I can't see how

To Autumn

learning to put a condom on a cucumber is going to help me in my future life.

We have breakfast, just toast today, and Grandma makes an announcement as I'm stuffing in the last mouthful.

"I am going to do my weekly shop today. I always do it on a Monday morning. I like to start the week being organised."

Great, just what I fancy. Hours wandering around a supermarket.

"Robyn, if you would like to go for a swim while I am shopping, you may. Annie, you'll have to come with me." I wasn't expecting her to offer this. For a second, I'm torn. I would love to spend the morning on my own, doing something I really enjoy, but the idea is shaded slightly, being at the expense of Anne's happiness. The guilt lasts only a few seconds.

"That's amazing, thanks, Grandma."

"As long as you promise to behave yourself. You're old enough, I think. If there's no problems and you don't cause any trouble, then maybe you and Anne can both swim in the pool without my supervision. If you don't do anything that will cause me problems."

It seems the older I get, the bigger the price becomes for these moments of happiness. My temporary independence in exchange for Anne's. When adults become nostalgic and make statements like claiming their teenage days were the best of their lives, they must be forgetting an awful lot of the shit they went through. Can't I just wake up tomorrow and be a grown up, these messy days behind me, and capable of dealing with whatever's thrown my way?

For now, I'll take this happy moment and live it guilt free. Tomorrow is my birthday, and I've had a crappy year. Being a teenager sucks pretty much all the time. I deserve a few moments of happiness, right? Why am I trying to justify it? Why is there always a nagging feeling that tells me I don't deserve it, that I should focus on making sure Anne's happy. I shut that voice down. Only for today.

Grandma asks me if I want anything special from the supermarket. I am too full of joy to be able to think of anything. I'll leave that to Anne.

†

"We'll be a good few hours. I like to go to several stores to make sure I find the best deals."

Take your time. "That's okay, Grandma, I'm happy to look after myself. I'll take my books and probably have a good long swim, too."

"Good girl. Be back here for lunch time then." Grandma and Anne leave, and the space stills. I want to check yesterday's paper before I make my way to the pool. It usually contains a TV guide for the week. I'm sure Dean said there was a TV room somewhere in the club house. If I'm lucky, I could find a way to watch *Neighbours* before Grandma gets home. Sometimes in the holidays they change the timeslot. I check the listing carefully, as I don't like to read the episode blurbs ahead of time, and it confirms a

To Autumn

schedule change for the next six weeks. The lunchtime slot will be showing a whole hour early, at half twelve. Just as well I checked. I might be able to make this work.

Then some preparation before I can go to the pool. I want to make sure I don't look as babyish as I did yesterday. First to go are the pink neon sunnies. I'll sit in the shade. I choose the plain navy tankini, the swimsuit that looks the least childish. My reflection is acceptable, and the two-piece appears to highlight my newly forming curves, whilst holding in my slightly wobbly belly, which is the look all the magazines say I should be going for. I chuck on a paisley sarong anyway. Mum's sarong. I'm sure she wouldn't mind me borrowing it for the holidays when she has no use for it. There's not a lot I can do about the sunhat Dad chose, but I am determined not to end up with a sunburnt head like I did in France last summer. Not only did it hurt like nothing else I've ever experienced – for a week – my scalp then flaked for nearly a month, making me look like the before side of a Head and Shoulders commercial.

Once I'm dressed, lotioned, adjusted and packed, then checked over twice, I head to the pool. I'm ready for a swim. I can't wait to transfer all the words I've swallowed over the weekend into a few lengths of front crawl. And maybe Autumn will be around, lifeguarding. It'd be nice to hang out together without Grandma and Anne there, bringing down the cool factor.

†

I walk through the turnstile, and clock two guys on duty with no Autumn to be seen. Oh well, I have *Oranges* to read and swimming to catch up on, and most importantly, some proper time alone. I'm exhausted from keeping up the constant pretence of being someone I'm not.

I find a spot near a row of girls who are doing their best Malibu Barbie impressions, jutting out their cleavage and hips in the eyeline of the two male lifeguards. I sit in their shade.

Even out of the sun, the day is warm, and the call of a swim is too inviting to ignore. I put away *Oranges* and walk to the edge of the pool. There's a narrow lane for swimmers sectioned off to the right-hand side. Not even a full-width lane, but enough to make a clear path for the whole length of the pool, if I can manoeuvre around the breaststroke brigade in their iced-gem caps. I climb down the metal steps and feel instant relief as my body sinks into the unheated water.

I quickly find a steady rhythm, freestyling up and down, finally clearing my mind of confusing and complicated thoughts. I haven't swum for a while, and it feels a bit like hard work to start with. Anne and I used to go every Tuesday after school and Sunday afternoons with Mum, and we'd have as long it would take Mum to swim a mile to play. Last year I started to spend more time swimming lengths with Mum though. I like the way I can forget everything and just be in the moment, and before long, an hour has passed. We haven't been back to the pool since Mum went into hospital. I haven't thought about how much I missed that routine, and the peace that swimming brings to my chaotic thoughts; how freeing it can be to have nothing else matter, even if only for an hour.

As I swim up and down this lane, thoughts are coming and going. I use the front crawl strokes to push them away. I zone out of the noise around me, the kids screeching, laughter and loud conversations. The water buoys me, and the familiar surge of energy kicks in once the initial shock of movement passes.

†

The pool starts to empty, and I realise that lunch time is approaching. The clock above the turnstiles reads quarter past twelve. Fifteen minutes until *Neighbours*. I hope I can squeeze in today's episode before heading back to Grandma's, if it's possible to use the rec room TV I've been told about.

I leave the pool area and head to the club house. I'm sure Dean said the rec room would be past the main entertainment lounge. The clubhouse is busy inside, and I can hear the kids club entertainers singing a song to their charges. After every line, a jumbled and out-of-tune repetition follows. I walk past the glass doors that open into the lounge, and the space becomes darker but noisier. A few metres farther down into the corridor, I meet some more glass doors, which are shackled with a heavy royal blue curtain.

I push my way through and find myself in another world that smells of sweaty socks. Electronic lights and sounds claim the space up front. Towards the rear of the room, there is a ragged pool table and two ancient ping pong tables. The smoking kid from the park and his mates are crowding round all three, claiming the only form of fun to themselves. Jamie is standing on the edge, looking quite discouraged at his chances of being allowed a game.

Next to the games is a make-shift seating area with some sofas, similar to those in the entertainment lounge. Similar, but drink-stained and cigarette-burned. Above these seats is a television smaller than the colour portable in my bedroom at home. While someone has switched it on, no one is watching the flickering and muted *Tom and Jerry* cartoon.

I walk towards the TV hoping to find the channel buttons, but I already know there's no hope for me. The pool players are being too loud to hear what my Ramsay Street friends are saying. As I reach the TV, I can't even see a remote control or a way to change the channel anyway. Defeated, I slink back out of the rec room. Might as well make my way to Grandma's to see if she and Anne are back.

†

I open the main entrance door, and seeing natural light again nearly blinds me, just as I am almost knocked over.

"Sorry!" says a familiar voice. "I'm in a hurry. I've only got about thirty seconds until *Neighbours* starts." Autumn.

"Oh, but the TV in the rec room is playing a cartoon. I couldn't see how to change it over," I say, trying not to sound too disappointed or desperate.

"Aha. Well, my love, I have the keys to the castle. As in access to the TV in the staff room upon which I laid claim to TV rights for this slot, on pain of death. I even managed, through some gentle persuasion, and winning a few games of poker, to bag the same slot for my lunch break."

"Oh well, lucky you. Enjoy!" I say and start to head back out of the door.

"Lucky me, yes, but would you care to join me? Beats watching it on my own. I'm guessing you're a steadfast fan if you were prepared to try and watch it in that grubby rec room?" I nod. "So, come on then, I'll sneak you into the staffroom with me."

Before I know what's happening, I'm following Autumn into a smoke-filled oasis. The room is little more than worn-out sofas, a vending machine, and the functioning TV she promised, but is, somehow, magic.

"Have a seat," Autumn says and points to the least threadbare couch, while she switches the clunky unit on. A couple of park staff are sitting at a table eating leftover pasta from Tupperware, but they don't pay any attention to us. I'm scared my cover will be blown and I'll be thrown out of here before the end of the opening credits. But they don't stir, and within seconds of sitting down, the cheesy but comforting lyrics about good neighbours becoming good friends are floating towards to my ears. I am home.

"Just in time," we say at the same time. Autumn laughs. I blush.

"So, you're up to date, right?" she asks.

"Yep. Never missed an episode. I even tape it on the days I'm not gonna be home from school on time. It didn't occur to me to check whether Grandma would have a TV or not, or I would've set something up at home."

"You can't call and ask the folks?"

"I'm the only one who can work the VCR," I say, glad I can sidestep the parent question.

"I'm chuffed they show it over here, even though I had to rewatch six months of episodes. It's the only thing I've found that makes me feel connected to home. I'm from the suburb where they film the show in Melbourne. I can walk to the real cul-de-sac where the street is set…okay shush, it's starting. I need to know about Lou and the stolen goods."

Wow, I never thought I would meet someone who takes *Neighbours* as seriously as I do.

"I started watching with my Mum when I was seven, and she was off work waiting to give birth to my sister. Mum said she thought Anne would come out singing the theme tune."

"Someone at uni told me a lot of babies recognise it when they hear it, because they heard it in the womb."

To Autumn

The sofa is not exactly large, and for us both to sit comfortably mine and Autumn's arms are touching. I'm finding it a challenge to concentrate on Toadie and Lance's antics and what Harold and Madge are up to today. The goose bumps forming on my skin take on a life of their own.

Autumn sinks further back into the sofa and her arm is even more closely pressed against mine. I lean forward, separating us so she won't notice the reaction I'm having. I can still feel her skin brushing mine after the contact has stopped.

When Beth and I kissed it was nice, pleasant, but there wasn't the kind of current I feel just being in the same vicinity as Autumn. I didn't know another person could do that to me. Does she feel it too? Why aren't the episodes longer than twenty-one minutes?

Too quickly, there's the cliff hanger ending on the screen. The staffroom door opens, and a group of lifeguards and clubhouse staff walk in, continuing an animated conversation. I miss the final line of the episode and then the closing theme music starts. Autumn stands up.

"You wankers, we missed the last lines," she says.

Her tone is more playful than the disappointment that is sweeping over me.

"You found another loser to watch that trash with, did you?" says the Leonardo DiCaprio lookalike who I'm sure is Autumn's boyfriend. Autumn turns to me.

"Ignore that melon. Look, Robyn, I'm here every day, same time same place. If you want to watch with me, that's cool. I've not had a *Neighbours* buddy in a while. No one back home watches it anymore, and my…friends here aren't interested either. It'd be nice to have someone to dissect the episodes with."

My stomach flips with butterflies, like it does the moment I coast on a wave into the shore. Of course, she's only interested in a viewing partner, I know that. But it doesn't stop the mix of adrenalin and sweat.

"Uh, sure. If Gran says that's okay and no one minds me being in here."

"Leave your grandmother to me, I know how to charm ladies like Mrs Gale," she says, as though the outcome is a fait accompli.

"Thanks. And I'd better be going back to the caravan, they'll probably be home now, and I should eat some lunch anyway. Starving." Stop rambling, Robyn!

"No worries. See ya later," she says. I stand up and we are facing each other. She leans in to give me a hug. I'm not the touchy feely type with my friends back in London. I just kind of stand there and then, as I'm about to hug her back, she pulls away, and I end up grabbing her arms instead. We look like we're squaring up to wrestle. She looks me in the eyes and smiles. I loosen my grip, expecting Autumn to do the same. I feel like she's reading me, the sentences of my life story. After a few more seconds she lets go. I turn to leave.

"Bye," I say, already on my way out of the door.

Chapter Eight

I return to Grandma's. A conversation is taking place, but I'm not able to make out the words. The voices hush to a whisper as Anne and Grandma see me arrive at the edge of the pitch. They look at each other, not doing a good enough job to disguise their conspiracy.

"Hi," I say. "I hope I'm not back too late. I found somewhere to watch *Neighbours*. Autumn said I could watch it with her every day if I like."

"Sounds wonderful, Robyn. She seems like a nice girl. Very polite. Ham sandwich for lunch? You're just in time. There are some things I need to do around the mobile home this afternoon, Robyn. Seeing as you made it back safe and sound from the pool, and I've had no reports of trouble, why don't you take Annie there this afternoon. As a trial. I'm sure Autumn will keep an eye on you both."

My lucky day. I wasn't expecting this show of trust from Grandma this soon. Anne's smiling, and with the chance of a swim, she's not even upset about being called Annie.

"Sure, shall we do the washing up first?"

"Oh, why don't you leave that for now and do all the dishes together tonight? You both did such a quick job of it yesterday, might as well just go the once. I'm sure you'd both prefer more time for fun?"

"If you say so! Thanks, Grandma. Okay, Anne, pack your swimmers and towel. You'll need your goggles as well, the chlorine's strong down there."

†

Autumn is sitting up on the lifeguard seat. She waves at us, and we find a spot in the shade to settle down. Purely a practical decision as I am not going to wear those kids' sunglasses, and absolutely nothing to do with the view of the lifeguard stand. Besides, I just want to read this afternoon, after my long swim this morning and I couldn't stop thinking about Jeanette and Melanie before I fell asleep last night. No wonder I'm having weird dreams.

†

To Autumn

"Woo hoo! Robyn, Annie!" The unmistakable caterwaul brings me out of *Oranges* and back to the poolside. The clock shows just after five. I've been reading and daydreaming for three hours solid. Anne climbs out of the pool where she's spent most of the afternoon playing with the inflatables.

"Hi, Grandma," I say, hoping she will pipe down. Not a good look to have your gran come and collect you. "I didn't know you were going to pop down. We're just about ready to leave."

"Hello, Mrs Gale." Once again Autumn has moved from nowhere in sight to by my side, before I even have a chance to gather my wits. Stealth ninja.

"Oh, hello, dear. Have my girls been any trouble for you today?"

"They've been perfect. In fact, Robyn was excellent company at lunch time." Once I have a good enough tan, I won't need to worry about uninvited blushing. Damn sitting in the shade.

"Did she tell you I invited her to join me every day?"

I'm not sure how comfortable I am having these two women talk about me as if I'm not even here. Anne is already walking towards the turnstile.

"Yes, dear. I suppose, as tomorrow is her birthday, she deserves a treat to watch her favourite TV show."

Thanks, Grandma. I'd planned to forget about my birthday this year. I'm not looking forward to celebrating it without Mum and Dad.

"Birthday, eh? The big One-Six?" Autumn says, with a twinkle in her eye. "Old enough to marry…"

"I guess I'll suddenly be an adult tomorrow. Overnight change to past-it? All downhill from here would you say?" There's only one way to reply to banter.

"Oh, I don't know, Mrs Gale. These young ones today don't have a clue, do they? Even if they do have great taste in books," Autumn says, before starting back to her chair. "See you at twelve-thirty then? I'll bring a pressie."

"What a nice girl, always polite," Gran says.

We pack up the rest of my stuff and head towards Anne.

"Robyn, I know these aren't the best of circumstances to be celebrating your birthday under, but I promise you that Anne and I will try and make it special."

"Thanks, Grandma, and you, Anne."

"Did you know you were born on Prince Charles and Princess Diana's wedding day? You were nearly called Di-"

"I know, Grandma," I say, and Anne takes hold of my hand.

"Probably just as well. She hardly behaves like a princess these days. Always on the front pages of the tabloids in her bikini, flaunting about on yachts with all manner of men. That sort of behaviour does not become a princess, not at all."

"Doesn't she deserve to be happy though?" I ask. I wouldn't have minded being named after a beautiful woman like Diana.

To Autumn

"It's those boys I feel sorry for." We reach the mobile home. "Okay, off you go to shower, girls, I'll start dinner."

Chapter Nine

I wake to the sound of scurrying coming from the living area, and a whispered set of commands. "Set the table. Pour the juice. Hold this." There's a crashing sound of something falling from the table to the floor. The whisper continues, "Shhh." I'm not in a hurry to get out of bed. More vivid dreams have exhausted me; I spent most of the night running away from a figure who sounded like Jeanette's mother but whose face alternated between Grandma, Autumn and Dean.

Once the noise settles, I make a loud song and dance of being awake and climbing out of bed. The flurry of activity in the living area gets louder.

To Autumn

"Just a second, dear," Grandma shouts. I wait, my hand on the doorknob. "Okay, you can come in!" I walk through to the living area and see that Grandma and Anne have made a good effort of it: some balloons, a birthday banner, juice on the table, and a Royal Wedding commemorative tea pot – which'd better contain tea and not just be on show as an anniversary celebration.

Anne points to a seat at the table, and I sit down. Grandma serves up scrambled eggs on toast with smoked salmon, my all-time favourite breakfast meal, and then she and Anne sit down with me.

"A toast," Grandma says. We all lift our juice glasses. "Happy birthday, my dear Robyn. I'm very glad to have you spending it here with me. I'm glad to have you both here."

Grandma pauses and for a second, she has the same look Dad has whenever he pretends he isn't crying. Then she gathers herself, and we clink our glasses together.

"Get stuck in girls, before it gets cold." I eat slowly, savouring the taste of fluffy eggs, and smoky salmon. Bliss.

When we finish, Grandma takes our plates over to the sink. "Annie and I put our heads together to find you a little present. I hope you like it," Grandma says, and Anne pulls out a perfectly wrapped package from behind her back. She hands it over to me, and I have a little feel.

"Go on then, rip it open, dear!" Grandma says and laughs. I don't want to rush. I prepare to put on my grateful face, however crappy this gift is going to be. I can't imagine Grandma would have any idea what to choose for me.

I carefully unstick the paper from the tape and unfold the ends, and then gently put my hand in to release the contents. Mum would expect me to try and save the wrapping paper for reuse, even though in sixteen years (sixteen, I can say that now!) I've never once seen her or Dad reuse wrapping paper.

I pull out a crumbling and dusty hardback book with the word "Letters" embossed on the mud brown front, followed by "John Keats." My English teacher told us about this book in school once, but I hadn't been able to find a copy of it at our local library.

"I went to a second-hand book shop in Totnes. Mr Hooper recommended the place," Grandma started. "The owner said that any Keats fan needs to have this book on their bookshelf. Although it doesn't look much, this is a second edition, from the 1930s. If you look after it, one day it might be worth something."

I'm lost for words. This is a perfect present.

"It's perfect. Thank you. Both! Very thoughtful." Grandma and Anne both stare at me, and I feel like a performing seal with a waiting audience, so I start to leaf through the book. It will be good to read more about the inspiration for my new favourite ode. My eyes start to water.

"No need to cry, dear. We just wanted to find something you would love."

"That book's very dusty, that's all, Grandma," I say. I'm categorically not crying.

"Of course it is, dear," she says. I blink away the tell-tale tears.

"Listen, I know you said this day might be difficult for you," Grandma continues, ignoring my protests, "what with your Mum… and Dad not here to celebrate with you…" I want to shout that I never said such a thing. Did I?

"But," Grandma persists, "we do have a little something from your father. Annie, pass the other present to Robyn. There's a good girl."

Anne pulls out a second, less well wrapped gift and a card. Dad must have hidden them in her rucksack.

I unwrap the present carefully again. To my surprise, I'm greeted with a new pair of sunglasses, mirrored Ray Bans. Way cooler than the neon pink disasters I've already discarded. Sweet.

I open the card, not sure what to expect, as all our Christmas and birthday cards usually come in Mum's handwriting. There's a brief message, "Have a great day, Love Mum and Dad x" scrawled in Dad's barely legible handwriting, and a £5 note. My eyes are watering again and this time I can't blame the dust. I put on the sunglasses.

"Very grown up, Robyn. I'm sure they will impress your new friends." Grandma gathers up the wrapping paper and tosses it all in the bin. "The day is yours to schedule, birthday girl. What would you like to do? The only thing I've arranged is a little birthday tea for you this evening, and I thought we could go to the bingo night at the club house later. I've invited that friend of yours and his family along, too. Dean, isn't it?"

My stomach does a little lurch, and the concrete lump, that I was beginning to think had vanished, makes its presence known. What on earth made Grandma do that? She looks pleased with herself. I can't think of much worse than spending a birthday evening playing bingo with a bunch of parents and grandparents, and a boy who might have hold of the wrong end of the stick about me.

"Sounds like fun, Grandma. Thank you." I try and handle the precarious situation with care. "Maybe we can go for a walk? I'd like to see farther along the beach if we can? As long as we can be back for lunch time?"

"Ah yes, your lunch date with Autumn and that TV show." Grandma chuckles.

We're not having a date. We're just two dedicated *Neighbours'* fans meeting up at a specific time to watch an episode together.

"So, can we do that? And maybe hang out by the pool this afternoon?" I ask. Anne smiles at me.

"A walk. Just like your mother. We can try, but I'm not sure how far these old bones will carry me. As it's your birthday, we'll see what we can do," Grandma says.

I'm pleased. Mum's the reason I like walking, but I can't help that.

"Okay, that's settled then. Why don't you and Anne pop down to the shower block, while I do the washing up?"

To Autumn

†

Grandma enjoys herself more than she's willing to let on during the walk, especially when we find a new tea shop she didn't know had opened, farther down the promenade. She takes respite, but allows Anne and me to walk farther, all the way up to the end of the bay.

When we return to Smugglers' Cove, I am covered in sweat and sand. I would like to clean myself up before I meet Autumn, but Grandma wants to check the post. I might have something from my school friends, so we join her. The post room is next to the reception desk which also doubles as the mini supermarket.

While we wait, I look at myself in the security mirror. With a tan forming, my new Ray Bans, and relaxed-but-windswept hair, a more sophisticated version of me than I am used to seeing stares back. I don't feel like I am her, yet, but I like the way she looks.

The clock above the Formica-coated reception desk, straight out of a wobbly *Crossroads* set, shows quarter past twelve. Almost time for *Neighbours*. As soon as Grandma's back, I'll go and look for Autumn. Anne is hovering by the penny sweets, and I decide to put my birthday money to good use.

"Choose whatever you'd like, Anne, on me!" She gives me a quick hug, then fills a small paper bag with a rainbow assortment of gummy sweets designed to make your teeth fall out. I pay, and then Grandma comes back round from the residents' pigeonholes. She's carrying several envelopes.

"These two are for you, Robyn," she says, and passes me a blue and a yellow envelope. I tell Grandma that I'll take them with me to open while I wait for Autumn, because I'm hoping the cards are filled with lots of juicy details of all the boys my friends have snogged. We agree to meet back at the caravan after the episode, for lunch.

"Lovely, see you in a bit, dear. Annie, you'd better come with me. I want to make sure you don't eat all of those sweets at once."

We leave the shop, and they head off together towards Grandma's caravan. Grandma helps herself to one of Anne's sweets and quickly stuffs it in her mouth before anyone else can see.

I walk towards the club house, which is just in front of the reception. Why do holiday parks always bunch their communal buildings too close together? Do they think it makes things more convenient? The only thing I've noticed is you spend the whole holiday bumping into the same people over and over again and end up pretending you haven't seen them or stuck in a polite conversation trying to think of a reason to escape.

I'm still a bit early, so I sit on the cracked wooden bench next to the club house door. The ground around it is covered in cigarette butts and gravelly sand. There's a constant flow of holiday park staff and kids in and out of the entrance door to the highlight of the park.

To Autumn

I pick up the blue envelope, which is addressed to me in Tanith's handwriting. The birthday card inside has a picture of the Spice Girls and a number six on the front. Inside, the printed message says: "Have a posh, sporty, baby, ginger, scary birthday." Only Tanith would choose a card like this, sending me something for a six-year-old in her twisted enjoyment of irony and teasing me.

She's written a lengthy note in the card. Reading that our plans to hang out by the Serpentine to scope boys haven't proved very successful is a bit of a relief. I'm not missing much. In fact, they're having a similar experience to me: "There aren't any piles of fit boys, only the pits of their spotty younger brothers and sisters." They're yet to find where the hotter boys are hanging out. And they miss me. The card is signed by both Tanith and Michelle, so I wonder who the other card is from.

The yellow envelope is addressed to me in shaky handwriting that is familiar, but not at all expected. Mum. I stare at the envelope, tracing my name. I don't know if I can open it. Not only has Mum not been able to say anything to me or Anne when we've visited her in hospital, she hasn't written anything to us either. These are the first words I've had directly from her since she was admitted to hospital three months ago. Is she better? Why didn't Dad tell us on Sunday if there's been a change?

I find it maddening that Dad doesn't trust me enough to handle important information and still treats me like a little kid. He should know by now I can handle the big stuff.

I've had to for months already and I haven't broken. Well not in a way that he knows about. I've had enough of sugar-coated updates about Mum. All that does is make things more confusing. And isn't her starting to improve good news? Why wouldn't I want to be told some good news?

My stomach swirls. The jumbled feelings spin around like concrete in a washing machine.

I unstick the envelope flap and take out the card, which isn't strictly a birthday card. The picture is a copy of a painting of two people swimming in the sea.

Inside, the writing is hard to read because it's quite shaky, but I can make out the words.

My darling girl, Robyn.

Not so much a girl anymore, as a woman, today. My little girl all grown up. My brave girl.

I want you to know I am thinking of you, always thinking of you and your sister. That's what keeps me going, what gives me hope I will recover.

I wish I had taken the time to tell you that you can be whoever you want to be, do whatever you put your mind to.

But you don't need to decide that right now. Take your time, don't rush. At 16 (16!) you don't need all the answers. I'm not sure any of us ever have them. And my love, you don't need to make decisions now that will affect your life forever, you have all the time in the world.

You mean the world to me.

All my love, my darling, darling daughter. Mum xxx.

To Autumn

Dad told us that she drove into the wall because she felt like she would never be the same again, that she couldn't cope with her medication still not working and her doctors not taking things seriously enough. Until it happened, Anne and I didn't know what was going on as Mum and Dad had kept it between themselves. I mean, obviously I knew something was wrong because she hadn't been the same old Mum for some time, and she started to spend more time in bed, some days only getting up to have a cigarette.

The day before Mum took Dad's car, when she found Beth and me kissing, we had a heart to heart, once she calmed down. She wasn't completely coherent, and I had to try and work out what she was saying. But the message was loud and clear, she wasn't happy about me kissing Beth and if I wanted to make her happy I should never do it again.

When I was little and fell down, or was upset about something, Mum was there to hug me and wipe away the tears every single time; I've always been able to tell her whatever's going on, whatever I'm feeling. Not being able to do that, not having her here for me, sometimes it feels like she died when she crashed that car. I don't know if I'll ever be able to tell her any of my problems ever again.

Then, suddenly, surprise! Here she is inside a birthday card, resembling the Mum I know. Following up on the conversation that ended mid-talk, as if she's only been away for a couple of days. A clear, flashing signal that I shouldn't allow myself to carry on the silly schoolgirl crush that's forming.

I put the card back in the envelope.

"G'day. Happy birthday, sweet sixteen." The concrete in my stomach swells like a stone sponge full of everything I don't want to be feeling. "Had a nice day? Lots of cards and pressies?" she says, nodding to the envelopes in my hand.

"I did alright. Ray Bans. An old edition of Keats' letters from Grandma." I don't feel like talking, and I wonder if she notices.

"Nice…the sunnies suit you." Don't blush, Robyn. "Maybe I could come over and take a look at that old edition? I've only been able to read the crappy paperback of the selected letters they have in the uni library."

I nod, not able to say no without looking like a twat.

"Well," Autumn continues, obviously not noticing my mood, "I have a little something for you. Not quite as exciting as my main man Keats though. I'll grab it from my locker after the episode."

A flutter of excitement, then I want to throw up. We walk into the building and I take deep breaths.

The staff room is quiet again. I ask Autumn if I can make myself a cup of tea, and she sets up the TV. I bring over a cup each and settle myself on the sofa. She joins me, and once again our sides meet in the middle. I try and lean to the left, towards the sofa arm, but that doesn't make any difference, and I just look like I'm fidgeting.

To Autumn

All through the episode, Mum's words play on repeat at high volume, and I'm not able to pay any attention to whether Toadie will report Lou's stolen goods to the police. Not even *Neighbours* can take my mind off things. Before I know it, the closing music is playing, and I've no idea what happened.

Autumn jumps up and bounces over to the set of battered lockers. She opens one and pulls out a small, nicely wrapped present.

"Here you go, sweet sixteen… something I thought you might like." She passes it over, and I start to unwrap it in my usual way.

Autumn laughs. "I haven't given you a stick of dynamite. You don't need to be delicate," she says. I forget that other people's parents don't make them open wrapping paper with the intention of saving it for never-reuse. I rip the last piece off to reveal a cassette. The cover bears a hand drawn cartoon of me, sitting at the pool reading with my headphones on.

"I made you a mixtape. You always have your Walkman on whenever I see you sunbathing. I thought you might like some new music to try. These are most of my favourites, but they're songs I think you'll like, too." I turn the case over and there's a handwritten track list on the back. "I've listed all the songs and the artists. Like I said, my favourites, and all the artists that are essential playlist material. If you know what I mean."

I don't know what she means. The list's mainly full of people I've never heard of, with weird names like Horse or Melissa Etheridge or The Indigo Girls or Ani DiFranco. There's a couple on there I do know though, KD Lang, Joan Armatrading and Dusty Springfield. They're all women.

A penny starts to drop. They're not just women, they're women with something in common, if comments my parents have made over the years are anything to go by.

"Are these all… lesbian singers?" I whisper.

"Absolutely. If you haven't heard of many, think of it as a starter list."

"But why would I want a lesbian singers starter list?" I ask, still whispering despite the panic rising quickly through me.

"Well, you know… because you're a…" Autumn cuts off, in response to the look of horror on my face, "woman."

"Do you think I'm a lesbian?" I ask, no longer holding a whisper. Still clutching the cassette, I run out of the room before she has a chance to answer.

On the way back to Gran's, I realise I left my birthday cards behind.

Chapter Ten

I'm furious at myself for leaving behind the only communication I've had from Mum in over three months. I'm furious at Autumn for jumping to conclusions based on what I read and a bit of blushing, and for giving me a present that's bloody obvious. What am I supposed to do with this cassette? I can't let anyone see it. The last thing I need after what Mum wrote in her card is a signpost telling the world who I am.

I sit on the steps of the caravan entrance. I'm covered in tears and sand dust, but I don't care who sees me. I consider throwing the cassette as far as I can, to stop it from taunting me anymore.

But something stops me. The detail in the cartoon drawing stares at me. Autumn had such a look of excitement on her face as she handed the present over. She said she'd chosen her favourite singers. Is Autumn a lesbian, too? No, there's no way. Whenever I see her with that guy, he has his hand on her back or around her shoulders. You'd only do that if you were a couple.

How can she possibly know that side of me? I've been working my hardest to keep it hidden. I've accepted that being attracted to women is something I'm not able to acknowledge. For Mum's sake, for her to be well again, I need to forget that part of me. If I'm giving out a dykey vibe without even realising it, how do I stop? What if someone else sees it?

Just because when I see couples in films kissing, I'd rather be the boy than the girl; just because when I'm near Autumn I feel like I'm going to implode with electricity, that doesn't mean I'm stuck being like that, does it? I can change it. I'll just have to find a way to show to everyone I'm not like that.

†

We spend the afternoon at the beach, rather than the pool, even though the weather is turning sour. Now I have a pair of sunglasses I'm proud to wear, I'm determined to rinse out every last drop of sun before the arrival of the heavy grey clouds that roll in one by one from the Channel.

To Autumn

I can't face reading Keats or *Oranges* today. They bring up replays of the scene at lunch. I told Grandma that I didn't want to bring my special new book to the beach in case it gets damaged. I listen to my Indie grunge collection, hoping the heavy melodies and ugly lyrics of Soundgarden, Nirvana, and Soul Asylum will obliterate any thoughts I have of Autumn.

The beach is quieter than it was on Sunday, fewer families frolicking about; no lifeguards playing bat and ball on their day off. I wander up to the tideline, but the water's too cold to swim in – I've not even stripped down to bikini level – even so, paddling is refreshing. The waves lap over my toes, and after a few minutes it stops feeling cold.

I finger the cassette from Autumn, which is still in my pocket, wishing I had the guts to throw it straight into the sea. Even if I can't live my life that way, will it always be a part of who I am? And what if people other than Autumn can tell? If there really is such a thing as a gaydar, will I always set it bleeping? Like being permanently attached to an airport security gate.

Maybe that's not even what Autumn meant; maybe I was the one who jumped to conclusions because I'd just read Mum's card. Maybe Autumn doesn't have a clue about me at all, and I've just made a tit of myself for no reason. And now I'll have questions to answer because I'm the one who said the word "lesbian." What if she tells Grandma?

I was crying when Grandma found me on the steps. I pretended it was because I was emotional about Mum's card.

She didn't pry. What a bloody way to spend my sixteenth birthday. None of this would've happened if Dad hadn't sent us here. None of this would have happened if Mum hadn't… turned our worlds upside down. What do you do when the person you go to for help becomes one of the reasons you need help?

    As the rain becomes too heavy for us to stay outside, I walk back up to where Grandma and Anne are planting a row of sand turrets around Grandma's deckchair. The three of us pack up. We walk home. Grandma asks us to shower and change anyway, as we have special birthday dinner plans and a call to Dad to squeeze in before that. I hope I can push the dark feelings down and pretend to enjoy tonight.

†

    I dress in the smartest outfit I brought with me, black skinny jeans, a white shirt and black waistcoat that Mum made for me for my birthday last year. This outfit is pretty much my uniform for parties and school discos. Although I probably look like I am trying too hard, the waistcoat makes me feel grown up. My DMs finish the outfit off. I consider sticking on my new Ray Bans as well, but as we're mostly going to be inside, I'll probably look like a dick. My hair as usual, can't be tamed however much mousse and gel I use, and the curls abandon me as though they would do anything not to be on top of my head. I put on one of Mum's chunky silver and amber necklaces that Dad said it was okay to

To Autumn

bring, as I reckon that will go well with the ensemble. I feel like I'm back in my own skin.

"Robyn!" says Grandma, with the same tone of disappointment Mum used to have when I was younger and wasn't happy with my appearance. Before she gave in to my tomboy tastes. "Don't you think a dress or skirt would be more appropriate? This is a special occasion, your special occasion, after all. Anne's dressed up." Anne is wearing a flowery number that I know she hates. It has the look of Grandma's influence about it.

"I didn't bring a dress or skirt with me." Not a lie, I don't have a dress or skirt in my wardrobe here or at home. "And this is my favourite outfit."

"I just don't understand young people today. You look lovely, dear, I suppose. Very… grown up." Nailed it. "Let's go, shall we? Don't want to miss our reservation or keep Dean's family waiting."

"Sure! Can't wait. You look lovely, too, by the way," I babble. "What's the menu like in the club house restaurant?"

"A mix of good old British cuisine: fish and chips, spaghetti Bolognese, curry, burgers. That sort of thing." I don't know why I asked, the menu's the same at all British holiday parks.

†

The queue at the phone box is long, just before dinner is peak time for calls home or to boyfriends and girlfriends left behind. I know we're going to be late for the reservation, but I'm not missing my call to Dad. While we wait, Grandma fusses over our appearances, trying to smooth down my hair and wipe an invisible mark from Anne's cheek. Finally, our turn. Grandma puts in two twenty pence coins before she starts the call. She dials unhurriedly, using her pocketbook again to find the number, and she gets through almost on the first ring. After a brief hello, she hands the phone straight to me. I pull Anne closer so she can hear as well. Grandma moves off to the side to give us some privacy.

"Hello, my darling. Happy birthday. Surprise!" I'm stunned to hear a voice other than Dad's at the end of the phone. It takes me a few seconds to register the voice that is the definition of home to me.

"Mum!"

"Did my birthday card arrive?"

"Yes, today," I say, shifting from foot to foot as I relive my humiliating scene with Autumn. How am I going to get my card back? "What are you doing…why are you home?"

"I've been allowed out for the first time. Permission from my psychiatrist. Just for a few hours. If it goes well, I'll be able to come out once a week, with your dad."

"Does this mean you'll be coming home soon?"

"I thought your dad would've told you about this, darling."

"No."

To Autumn

"I began a new treatment last week and for the first time something seems to have had an effect."

"What treatment? I didn't know there was another option," I say.

"The doctors say I won't be fully recovered overnight. If it works, it will take some time. Maybe your dad can explain better than me another day. I just wanted to say happy birthday in person." I can hear her breathing deeply, and she starts to sound tired.

"Well, I didn't want to raise your hopes, and I wanted it to be a surprise for your birthday, Robyn," Dad's voice pipes in from the background.

"Is Anne there?" Mum asks. Anne nods.

"Yes, she is. She's right here next to me. I can't believe we're talking to you. I wasn't sure…" I trail off, not wanting to make Mum feel bad that I'd started to believe we might never speak to her again.

"You weren't sure you'd ever be able to speak to me again? That I'd be silent forever?"

"It doesn't matter. We're speaking to you now. This is the best birthday present ever," I say, and Anne bounces up and down excitedly next to me. She's the most animated I've seen her since Mum went into hospital. "Anne's really excited too."

"Can I speak to my little Annie?" Only Mum is allowed to call her Annie. "Can she hear me?"

"She's right here, Mum. She can hear you." I pass the handset to Anne. After a minute, she hands it to me. "Me again, Mum. I don't think we have long left on the call."

"I just want you to know, I meant what I said in the card. I love you, and so does your dad," Mum says.

I just about fit in a "love you too" before the pips start. I hang up, unsure what to feel. I've wanted this for ages, to hear Mum's voice sounding normal again, to talk to her, to have her finally starting to recover. I should be happy.

The three of us start walking towards the clubhouse. Grandma is chattering away to Anne about how nice it is that we spoke to Mum, and how good for us and Dad if she's able to come home. I can't connect to any of it.

†

Dean and his family are already in the restaurant when we arrive. To my horror, we're shown to the table by Autumn's boyfriend, the guy that can't keep his hands off her. He is handsome like one of those non-singing boyband members with vacant expressions. With his blonde side sweep haircut (rather than the usual curtains look) and ironed uniform, he looks "dapper" as Grandma tells him. On top of that, he charms Grandma all the way to the table with his "yes ma'ams" and "whatever I can do for yous" no doubt a favourite of all the older ladies in the park.

"Isn't he a dish?" Grandma says as he leaves us to browse the menu, but she seems to be aiming the comment towards Mrs Jackson rather than me. Thank goodness.

Dean stands up to greet me. A drop of sweat sits above his eyebrow, and he leans in to give me a hug. I respond rather than end up in another wrestling hold. He gestures to the empty space next to him and I don't really have a choice, without coming across as difficult, other than to sit there. Jamie shoves over, and Anne squeezes in next to him on the other side of the round table.

Dean has dressed up for the occasion, wearing a suit jacket that is too big for him and a white shirt that looks very similar to mine. His dark afro curls gleam with the large volume of wet-look gel he has used to hold them in place. They're better behaved than my curls. We all say awkward hellos, except for Anne, who does at least wave when Grandma introduces her, and then we pick up our menus for something to do.

"I'm having the rump steak," Dean says confidently, and nods at his dad, as though they have discussed this in advance. "What do you fancy, Robyn?" he asks, his cheeks reddening.

"Spag bol – spaghetti Bolognese is my favourite, I'll have that, please," I say, and put the menu down.

Blondie comes over and takes our orders. I choose a lemonade to drink, even though Mum and Dad said I could have wine with my meals once I turned sixteen. I'm gonna assume Grandma wouldn't approve. No one else has ordered wine, and I'd rather not embarrass myself and try to order from the wine list. I wouldn't know where to start.

"Do you have a girlfriend, young man?" Grandma asks Blondie.

He blushes, as do I, already knowing the answer. He rebuffs her by responding, "Many. Why, should I tell them they have competition?" Sleaze.

All through dinner, Grandma and Mrs Jackson see how far they can push the flirting. Mr Jackson talks with Jamie and Anne, trying to ignore their remarks. Dean asks me questions about my life and growing up in London. I give one-word answers and don't ask any questions of my own.

We're about to order dessert when Grandma gives Blondie a wink and a nod. Before I have time to cringe, she, the rest of my tablemates, and the waiter are singing "Happy Birthday" as he carries over a chocolate cake with sixteen candles melting into the buttercream. People at the other tables turn around to stare, a few also joining in. It takes me three attempts to blow out the candles while everyone "Hip hip hoorays." I just want to crawl under the table.

†

Once we've finished our cake and Blondie has cleared away the plates, Grandma invites the Jacksons to join us for bingo and Mrs Jackson responds for everyone with an emphatic yes. We walk as a group to the club room, and Dean stands close enough that with each step his shoulder bumps mine. There are no goose bumps as our bodies make contact.

To Autumn

"We'll go to the bar," Dean offers, as the adults sit down. "Come on Robyn," he says, taking a tenner from his dad and dragging me towards the bar. "There's a little birthday surprise for you, Robyn," he says, in a whisper. Not another surprise, no thank you.

We order the round, and Dean taps his jacket. When the server has his back turned, Dean takes out a hip flask from an inside pocket and pours generous amounts of a clear liquid into our cokes. The server turns around before I have a chance to comment, and Dean pays the guy and asks for a tray.

"Vodka," he says quietly to me, quite proud of himself.

For the first time since the staff room, things feel like they are going in the right direction for a birthday celebration.

"Nice one," I reply, happy to be complicit. I take a big swig, nearly downing the half pint of coke and paint-stripper vodka in one.

"Woah, hang on. Let's buy you another coke so you don't run out."

"Thanks," I finish off the glass, "best present of the day." Dean smiles, hands me the tray and goes back to the bar. The vodka has an immediate effect, and I lose my balance, causing the drinks to spill. "Oops," I say to no one.

"Careful there," that familiar honey-dew voice says from behind me.

Shit. She's here.

"Just lost my balance," I mumble out.

"You forgot these," Autumn says, holding up my birthday cards, "when you ran off earlier. I…"

"Here you go," Dean takes the tray and hands me a drink. "Come on, we'd better take these over to the folks and your granny."

I smile at Autumn and offer my free hand for the cards. She puts them in my hand but doesn't unclasp her own.

"Thank you for looking after them," I say, my dry mouth making the words a husk. Dean's nudging me with the tray. "We need to take the drinks to our families before the bingo starts."

"You don't have to worry. Who do you think is calling the numbers?" Autumn laughs, still not letting go of the cards. "I wanted to check you were okay."

"Of course!" I squeak. "Why wouldn't I be?" I take a big swig of my enhanced coke. Autumn looks towards Dean, who is waiting for us to finish our conversation, and not about to leave without me. "So… cheers. Good luck." I pull on the cards and she releases them. The momentum causes me to stumble again. "Come on Dean," I say and turn away from her to walk towards the booth.

†

"Queue was there?" Mr Jackson asks when we arrive back at the table. He grabs his pint of lager and gulps a big mouthful.

To Autumn

"Sorry, Autumn stopped to speak to us."

"Lovely girl," says Gran. "Australian. Isn't that right, Robyn? A lifeguard. You should've asked her to join us." Dean looks panicked for a second.

"I couldn't, she's calling the numbers."

"Ah, well I can see why, with a voice like that!" Grandma says.

"Sorry, I spilled some of the drinks. The tray was heavy," I say, trying to move the conversation on.

A voice blares out from the stage. Mr Hooper. "Right now. Ladies. Germs. Boys and girls. My glamorous assistants will shortly be wandering around ready to sell you all the bingo cards you could ever need. Remember, one of those cards will be the winner! Fifty pence for one or four pounds for a book of ten. Can't say fairer than that, can I?"

Grandma buys a book and reluctantly tears a strip off for me and Anne. "You do know how to play bingo?"

"Dad used to take us," I say and Grandma hands us each a dabber. Anne immediately stamps hers on her hand but stops when she sees the look on Grandma's face.

Everyone gets comfortable around the table, laying out their cards, and we joke about how we might spend the twenty quid prize money.

"More bingo tickets," says Jamie.

Dean leans into me and whispers, "I'd take you out for a meal." I give him a smile, and he doesn't pull back, meaning he is sitting almost on top of my right side.

115

I can feel eyes on me, burning a hole into the back of my neck.

"Oooh. Looks like we're starting," Grandma announces to the table.

"Hello, hello. Didn't think I'd be back up here this soon," the honey-dew voice blasts through the mic. "Well, let's not hang about, shall we? I hope you don't mind if I throw in the odd Australian bingo call to mix things up?"

The ball machine whirrs to life and for the next twenty minutes, a stillness takes over the room, disrupted only by the occasional "shhh" and Autumn's announcements of the numbers.

I'm close to marking a line, but a man's voice calls for it while I still have one to go. We're on for a house. The concrete block starts to squeeze inside my stomach, when I reach two off winning. Winning would mean having to go up on stage to collect the prize from Autumn in front of everyone.

"Sausages on a barbie, number eleven," she calls.

"Hey," Dean shouts, before lowering his voice, "You're down to one to go." The faces around our table look up.

"I'm not even close," says Grandma with a hint of disgust. "Must be birthday luck."

"Twenty-three." All their faces look at me. I shake my head. "Six." Oh no.

"House! House!" Dean is calling up to the stage, waving my card.

To Autumn

"Looks like we have a winner from the lovely Gale table. Want to come up here young man, we need to check those numbers."

"Oh, I haven't won," he says edging out of the table to let me out. "The birthday girl has." Perfect.

"No, that's okay. You take the card up, if you want," I'm saying before I even realise it. I don't want to go up on the stage and have everyone stare at me. I don't want to be forced to talk to Autumn.

"I'll go up with you," he offers, which I can't really turn down.

"Okay then, now or never, Birthday Girl. Come on up and claim your prize. I promise I won't bite." A smatter of laughter passes through the room.

I take Dean's hand and climb up the stairs to the stage.

"Now, that wasn't too bad, was it? A round of applause for Robyn, everyone." Dean squeezes my hand. Autumn retrieves the prize money envelope from the table behind the ball machine. "Here you go. You can buy yourself a big birthday treat."

"Thank you," I just about stutter, and as I look down at all the faces, the effect of the vodka starts to take hold. I sway, losing my balance and the envelope. Autumn is down and picking it up before I blink. She hands it over and guides me off the stage.

"Right, time for a break ladies and gentlemen. Get yourselves to the bar."

†

"I want some fresh air," I say when we're back at the table, desperate to take myself out of the club house and out of sight for a minute. I'm keen to gather my thoughts. "Has it suddenly turned really warm in here?" I give the envelope to Dean. "A round of drinks on me," I add, then head for the door.

Outside, the rain has brought a coolness to the air this evening that is welcome. It hits my sweaty skin and after a minute my body temperature starts to return to normal. Families pass back and forth through the door, but out here, no one is paying me any attention.

Then after a few minutes, I hear, "I told your gran I'd come and look for you." Autumn. "You okay?" She walks up next to me.

"Yeah, of course I am. Why wouldn't I be?" I can't look her in the eye, instead facing straight ahead, with her to my side.

"Well, I'm not one to judge, but I'd say… cheap vodka, too much cake and… teen angst. They don't make good bedfellows."

"What do you know about it?"

"More than you might think. I'm sorry if I offended you earlier."

"Here you go, Robyn, another coke? Thought you might need a drink." Dean's voice cuts in between Autumn and me.

"Thanks, Dean. That's perfect. Just needed to cool down a bit. I'm ready to go back in."

He ignores Autumn completely. "We could stay out here, just the two of us, if you like."

"I'm sure your gran would want you to head back in, Robyn," Autumn says, a strained tone in the trail of her words.

I take Dean's hand again. "Yeah, I'll be there in a minute," I say. Dean laughs.

"Sure, I'll see you both inside. Have fun." Autumn turns around and walks back into the building. Out of the corner of my eye, I can tell she's looking at us through the glass door.

Dean pulls me towards him, so we're facing each other. He looks me in the eyes, and I can hear his quick, shallow breaths. Feeling Autumn's eyes still on us, I lean forward and kiss Dean. He tastes of the cheap vodka and extra strong mints. How long do I have to wait before I can politely pull away?

Chapter Eleven

Last night Grandma agreed that I could join the Jacksons at the pool again while she takes Anne on a secret mission for the morning. I wasn't involved in the decision because it happened when I was kissing Dean outside the club house. By the time we pulled up for air, Autumn wasn't anywhere to be seen and Jamie was coming to find us.

I drink five thimble sized glasses of water once Grandma and Anne have left. My head is pounding from the vodka, and I don't want to be sunbathing and making awkward conversation with Mr and Mrs Jackson while nursing this hangover. Maybe Grandma has some aspirin?

I push open her bedroom door, which is kept firmly shut twenty-four seven. The bed is made neater than any bed

To Autumn

I have ever seen. In the tiny bedside table there's a pharmacy's worth of pills. Right at the back are some aspirin, the soluble kind. Gross.

I have to split them across two thimbles of water but by the time I'm dressed to leave for the pool, I'm starting to feel human again.

With my books, my towel, my sunscreen, and some cash for a can of pop, I take one last look in the mirror and decide I don't look too awful. Passable thanks to the Ray Bans. Not that I am trying to impress anyone. I walk as quickly as is possible in flip flops on an uneven surface and arrive at the turnstile just as a blister is starting to form around the plastic thong between my toes. I take them off.

As I am pushing through the gate, the lifeguard whistle blasts, announcing my arrival. I walk to the poolside and curl my toes over the lip. My stomach dances with excitement and fear. I can't wait to swim, and as much as I long to see Autumn in her Baywatch-red swimsuit, I know I shouldn't feel this excited about it. I don't want to have these kinds of feelings about her. None of my other friends have to deal with this. Yet, I can't seem to stop it from happening. Why can't Autumn be a guy? That would make things a lot less complicated.

I'm starting to sweat under the weight of an existential crisis and the warmish sun, and then out of nowhere, a large splash of water rises up from the pool and soaks me. My towel and my Keats, and also the library copy of *Oranges* slipped inside, are drenched. The splash is followed by a wet Dean, who is laughing, and tries to give me a slippery hug.

"I didn't think you were going to notice me. You were miles away," he says, his version of an apology.

I pull away, mostly bothered that he's making the books even more wet. They'll take ages to dry out and the pages will warp. That's why I'd never bring my special edition to the pool, and I should have thought the same about a library book. Perhaps this is a sign to put it away and give up trying to read it. I could cope with losing a £1 paperback of Keats' poems but not a library book that would be tricky to explain away.

"You okay?" he asks. But doesn't wait for an answer. Instead, he points to a collection of towels and his parents and says, "You should sit with us if you're on your own." I can't bring myself to say that I was looking forward to being on my own. "Come and join us in the pool once you've dropped your stuff off."

"Okay. But I'll stay in the shade. I'm feeling a bit rough after your present yesterday." I'm never keen on anyone ordering me around like that, but I walk over to where he has pointed, flapping the drips off my book as best I can. Dean's parents look up and say a bright hello that I'm not able to match in response.

"Recovered from your big day, Robyn?" What does Mrs Jackson know? I'm more grateful than ever for sunglasses to hide behind.

"Err…"

"It must have been strange not having your parents here for your birthday. I didn't have a chance to ask Gloria why they aren't here as well."

"They're away for work, right, Robyn?" Dean jumps in. I'd forgotten I'd said that to him. Need to keep my stories straight.

"Yes… Dad had some business abroad and Mum went with him. That's why we're at Grandma's."

I take my time setting my towel and bag down. I try and place the towel close enough not to be rude, but not quite next to them, so I can try and read in peace. I scooch up against the fence to sit more comfortably and to have a clear view of the whole pool area. Dean turns and runs back towards the pool.

"Come in for a swim with us!"

"That must be a nice break for your parents. I wish the boys' grandparents were hands on."

With a smile, I flop down onto my towel, reapply my sun cream, then lean casually back against the fence.

"We have extra drinks if you need anything," Mrs Jackson says. Mums can't stop being mums, can they?

"Thank you, that's really nice of you to offer. I'm okay for now." I pick up the Keats and find a dry section to leaf through. I hold it slightly above my head so a little bit of sun can have a go at drying the pages, and then I can take a sneaky peak around me.

I wave at Dean and Jamie who are messing about in the pool. With the intention of being super casual, I take a side eye scan of the lifeguard area. Autumn is there, on her seat, looking right at me. I look back to the Keats and try my hardest to focus on at least one line of verse, but all the words are swimming up around me. I'm sweating more than the British summer time sun has the power to cause. And now I can't look back at her, just in case she is looking at me still. I hope she didn't see Dean ruining the Keats. Not that it matters what she thinks. Well, I've shown her who I really am now, there's no need for any more confusion.

I feel the icy glare of her eyes on me. My head is throbbing and the odes are dancing around on the page, impossible to read. The only way out of this situation is to put the book down and jump in the pool. That might freshen me up a little. And, at least from there I have a reason to have my head up and looking round, and if she happens to come into my eyeline, well then, that's not my fault, is it? Does everyone have a running narrative in their head, trying to justify every action they take?

I remove my sarong and stand up, which catches Dean's attention.

"Finally taken your nose out that book?" He shouts at me. Clearly, he's been waiting for the opportunity.

"Nothing wrong with a bit of reading to relax, before some exercise…" I'm such a nerd. "Okay, I'm coming in."

I walk around the wet concrete that surrounds the pool, towards the deep end. There's a crappy looking shower, not dissimilar to the shower block units. I rinse the sweat and sun cream off, just as the signs pinned to the fences tell me I must do. Yep, the poolside shower is not heated and has even less pressure than the showers in the central block. The rough-looking tiles that line the pool have seen better days, but they are clean enough. The water looks half chlorine, half pee this morning, but beggars can't be choosers and if I want to swim, I'll just have to deal with it. I'm sure most pools have the same chemical makeup. I find a bit of space and dive in, barely disturbing the water, just to show off. The lifeguard whistle blows loudly. Oops.

"No diving! No matter how slick you think you are." Well.

Dean sidles up. "She's got a right stick up her arse, that one," he says, nodding in Autumn's direction. "Thinks she can sing, too."

"I guess that's what she's paid to do. Can't blame someone for doing their job. Race ya. To the shallow end and back. Loser buys an ice cream."

He grins, obviously thinking it will be easy to win against a girl. Little does he know that Dad's owed me ice creams for the last three summers.

"Ready, set, go." He starts on set, but it doesn't matter, I know I can catch him. I'm already ahead before the turn, and although there is a bit of a challenge racing in a pool full of other people, they do make room for us. I don't even pause as I go under for the turn, and I'm already on my way back while Dean is still trailing his arm to the shallow end edge. I ease up, to shrink the gap between us, and let him almost catch me. Dad says that there's nothing worse than a bad winner, and that I have a tendency to be smug, so I try really hard to play it cool. If Dean is like any of Michelle and Tanith's boyfriends back home, his pride will be wounded if he's beaten by a girl.

"You didn't tell me you were an Olympic swimmer," he says, hiding his embarrassment fairly well, and without too much defensiveness.

"Three-time gold medallist. In the Gale family summer swim off, that is."

"Right. Well, all that competition has paid off."

"I just love to swim," I say. I don't add, "and show off." I can definitely feel another pair of eyes on me, but I control the urge to see where it might be coming from.

"I guess I owe you an ice cream," he adds, but the idea no longer sounds as fun as I thought it would. I would like to be eating ice cream with someone else entirely.

"I'm gonna swim some laps," I say, and swim off into the marked lane, before Dean can ask to join me.

After twenty lengths I climb out, my fingers are beyond prunes at this point, and head back to my towel.

"Would you like to join us for lunch, Robyn, there's plenty of sandwiches," Dean's mum offers. Dean rolls his eyebrows at his mum, but then smiles at me, looking hopeful I will join them.

"Oh, thank you, but Grandma said to be home for lunch. Maybe next time." I give myself a token wipe with the towel, then shove everything in my bag and put the sarong back on. It sticks to my wet legs as I walk to the gate. The

To Autumn

lifeguard's whistle blows, and I look back expecting to see Autumn on the other end of it, but instead there's a bloke. She is nowhere to be seen, but the clock reads quarter to one. She didn't ask me if I wanted to watch *Neighbours* with her today.

†

When Grandma and Anne come to find me, later than I expected, I am definitely ready to leave. They've been gone a while, and I'm glad the Jacksons had those extra sandwiches.

"We've a surprise for you, Robyn," Grandma says, jiggling a shopping bag in my direction, with an unusually big glint in her eye. More surprises? I don't think I'm capable of handling anything else right now. "Don't worry, I think you'll like this surprise."

"I'll just pack up my things," I say. I turn to the Jacksons. "Thanks for letting me sit with you, and for lunch."

"Has she been good?" Grandma asks. Just when you think adults can't be any more cringe.

"Of course," Mrs Jackson says and laughs as I roll my eyes when my back is turned to Grandma.

"Let's go," I say, keen to end this interaction quickly. Autumn is still lingering round the pool, and I don't want Grandma to decide it would be a good idea to strike up a conversation with her.

Back home I strip out of my pool gear and into trackies. Anne and Grandma wait for me in the lounge. I step back into the room and Grandma has laid out the items from the shopping bag.

"We are going to enter Annie in the Thursday night fancy dress costume competition." This really is a surprise. I had no idea there even was a fancy dress costume competition. I am glad Grandma said "Anne" and not, "both of you."

"Sounds…fun?" I say in a statement that is more of a question.

"She'll be going as the little matchstick girl," Grandma continues, ignoring my confusion. I look at the clothes laid out on the sofa. There's white leggings, a white long sleeved T-shirt and a pink swimming hat.

"Where's the costume then?" I ask, imagining some sort of rag-themed ensemble.

"Here. She'll wear the white clothes over her body, and the swimming cap, and she'll look just like a match. The little matchstick girl, see?"

I do see. The idea is kind of genius, kind of bonkers.

"I've been dreaming this up ever since your dad asked me to have you. I've always wanted to enter someone in the competition."

Anne is smiling, which I hope means she hasn't been coerced into this bizarre concept.

"Very inventive," I say, hoping it sounds like a compliment.

"Exactly, a winning strategy. Right, Anne, let's try everything on and see what we're working with." Grandma shoos Anne into her bedroom and behind the door I hear some rustling. They come back out.

"Ta-dah!" Grandma says. Anne walks forward. I have to admit, there is a look of a matchstick going on. The pink swimming cap really works. I adjust it a little, to help it sit on her head without creases.

"We should use talc," I say, unexpectedly becoming both excited and protective towards Anne. "It'll make it easier to put the cap on and we could try and match her skin colour to the clothes.

"Great idea, Robyn!" Grandma says.

†

The fancy dress costume is the opener for every Thursday's club house entertainment. Afterwards, the band play some mellow tunes. Apparently, this is something holiday guests look forward to and plan for during the run up to their stay. There are two categories: five and unders, and six and overs. Unsurprisingly, the over-sixes' group is much more popular and by the looks of it taken much more seriously. The five-and-unders' strategy appears to be about playing to the cuteness factor.

We arrive at the club house early, to register. Anne is given a number to safety pin to her costume. The idea is that in their two cohorts, each contestant is asked to do a circuit of the dancefloor, then front and centre for a full twirl. A panel of judges then score the contestants. Very simply, the winner is the contestant with the highest score. In the event of a tie, the head judge casts the final vote. Mr Hooper is hosting this debacle, so he can't be a judge. My stomach falls when I see the panel. The house band's guitarist, the woman from the shop, and Autumn are sitting at the judges' table. I wonder whether this will go in Anne's favour or not.

I buy us some drinks and we sit at our booth, Anne's costume hidden under a coat, in case of corporate espionage. The under sixes go first. There aren't many of them. They struggle with the instruction of circling the dance floor, and more than half are accompanied by a parent or older sibling. They are very cute though. A homemade Bagpuss is the best costume, in my opinion. The quality of costumes is serious.

After a short interval, the over sixes are ready to start. I'd say Anne is by far the oldest contestant. All seven of them, five girls, two boys, line up next to the stage and are called in number order. If the wee ones' level of seriousness was something to laugh at, this is next level competition.

Two Disney princesses are up first, a Belle and a very clever Ariel, with full on mermaid tail. Anne's facing stiff competition here. Then there's Woody from Toy Story in a home-made cowboy outfit, perfectly matching the character, complete with ANDY written on his boot, which he shows us during his spin around.

Anne's turn. Hopefully we haven't been too controversial going against the Disney grain. She steps out and Mr Hooper explains her title. "This is a conceptual costume, named The Little Matchstick Girl." The audience –

primarily parents of the kids entering – laugh and someone at the back applauds loudly. Could this idea actually work?

The final three kids finish their turns. Once they have all finished, the judges are still heads together discussing the scores.

"We'll leave you to go to the bar while the judges come to an agreement on the winners," Mr Hooper says jovially. I order another round of drinks, and Anne comes back to join us. The judges are still discussing the results. Mr Hooper walks over to them, and points to his watch. The whole event is supposed to be finished by 8pm so the rest of the entertainment can start.

Finally, he walks back to the stage, a piece of paper in his hand. The judges head over to the bar to pick up their own drinks.

"Right then, ladies and gents. The lucky winner of a ten-pound voucher to spend at any of Smugglers' Cove's outlets in the five and unders category is Brian the Bagpuss. Lovely work."

Brian's Mum goes up to receive the voucher. Then she and Brian are forced to have their photograph taken by the resident photographer.

"Photos for the winners' hall of fame," Mr Hooper declares.

"Now, next we have an unprecedented scenario. The judges have chosen a winner, however there was a tie between two of the contestants. Therefore, we have decided, for the very first time, to award a 'Judges' honourable mention' which will earn a five-pound voucher. This will be awarded to little Annie Gale, whose costume is the most inventive the judges and I have ever seen. Well done, Anne!"

    She has to go up to collect the voucher and have her photo taken. Grandma and I cheer wildly, and I am full of pride for them both. The outright winner is Woody. Quality but unoriginal.

    Once the judges' table has been returned to its usual place, Autumn slopes out, not even turning to look at me.

Chapter Twelve

Is it me, or do the days start to roll into one when they consist of pretty much the same activities with minor variations? How can it be another Saturday already? Another evening where I'm forced to smile all night and pretend to enjoy myself at the clubhouse, while I try and hide from Autumn.

Since my birthday I've managed to avoid interactions with Autumn. I've just about figured out her work schedule, and that means I can suggest to Grandma when we go to the beach and when we go to the pool without worrying about bumping into Autumn. A couple of times I've seen her wandering about the holiday park, but she's always been with other people, and I've managed to stay out of her eyeline. I'm just mortified that she would give me a present like that. What if Grandma had seen it? Not that Grandma would necessarily make the connection about the singers on the mixtape.

The cassette is under my pillow for now. I move the hiding place around to stop anyone finding it. Mum always knew exactly where to pinpoint my contraband, so I had to develop this tactic to stop her reading my diary. As much as the cassette represents everything that I am trying to forget about my life, I can't bring myself to throw it away. Like the Winona Ryder posters under my bed at home. I'm never going to look at them again, just in case it makes Mum try something stupid again, but I'm not ready to put them in the bin either. They are part of me. Just not a part I can ever share with anyone else.

†

I've actually enjoyed having Dean around. He's helped make it easier to forget about making a fool of myself and instead feel like I can just put that mess behind me. On the rainy days, and there's been quite a few, he's brought over Jamie and joined us in the caravan to play board and card games. This has meant we have expanded our playing options beyond Pass the Pigs and Uno for which I am very grateful.

Last night we hung out at the club house disco. Grandma let me go on my own because she can't stand the loud pop music being played. Dean and I danced, but not together, more like in a big group with some of the other kids from the playground. Friday night is the one night they ditch the warm cider for warm coke and a spinning disco ball. The DJ, Kev, is interesting. He wears a colourful jacket and every few songs mentions how "hip to the jive" he is. However, being a holiday park disc jockey on a Friday night doesn't really scream hip. He does play some good music though, and we danced to some proper tunes. My favourite is "Professional Widow" by Tori Amos. Thankfully Kev doesn't take requests or play slow numbers, which means I didn't have to negotiate an awkward slow dance with Dean.

Autumn was there for a bit, with her holiday park staff buddies. They are all old enough to buy real drinks at the bar, and it didn't take long for them to become loud and obnoxious. She didn't try and talk to me though.

†

Grandma has been teaching me the card game called bridge. I think she is missing being able to play with Mr Hooper and her other pals as often as she would normally when Anne and I aren't here. We can't play properly with just the two of us, but she's managed to teach me the basics. There's talk of Mr Hooper and another old timer coming over to give me a real game one of these days.

Anne has become really good at word searches which means she hasn't been forced to join in with us. Although I'm having something to talk to Grandma about, it also means she doesn't ask too many questions about Dean and

Autumn. She didn't mention it when I stopped watching *Neighbours* with Autumn. I've accepted that there'll be five weeks' worth of episodes I'll never see. On Saturdays, the new TV guide arrives with the newspaper – turns out that Grandma buying the *Daily Mail* has one advantage – and at least I can read the episode descriptions and sort of keep up with what's happening on Ramsay Street.

She'll be back any minute, so I should finish the bacon sandwiches. I think Grandma has become a bit more relaxed about when we can have a treat for breakfast because I am actively involved in the cooking and cleaning up. I turn off the grill and finish buttering the toast while the tea is steeping. Anne has set the table and adds the ketchup, just as Grandma walks in with zero sweat broken despite her power walking ensemble.

†

We sit down to eat. Right when I've just planted my whole mouth with the first bite, Grandma starts a conversation.

"Mr Hooper's confirmed our fourth for bridge, Robyn. I've invited everyone over for a game tomorrow evening. We'll have supper first. Everyone knows this will be your first game, so you don't need to worry about playing well. See it as a chance to practice, without any pressure."

My mouth is too full to answer. I put the sandwich down and offer a thumbs up in agreement. To be honest, tomorrow night and playing bridge well or not isn't high on

To Autumn

my list of worries. First of all, I have to run the gauntlet of being in the club house tonight, hoping that Autumn isn't performing or isn't there at all, really. Then there's Dean. Ever since we kissed, he's assumed we'll probably kiss again, and I'm running out of excuses that stop me finding myself alone with him. And then there's the creeping dread of exam results day. Every day that passes is one closer to the news being broken that I'm a big lying failure. Dad has been making some suggestions that he might go and pick up the grade slips from school on the Big Day (as he likes to call it) and drive them down for me. While I would absolutely love to have a visit from him, and spend time with him in person rather than at the other end of a pay phone, I'd rather not have to see the look on his face when he opens the envelope to a disappointing set of grades and what a disaster I've made of everything.

"Great," I say once the mouthful is chewed.

"I'm pleased you like the game, Robyn. Your Aunt Di and I used to play all the time with Mr Hooper. It's been a long time since I picked up the cards. There hasn't really been anyone I wanted to partner with since she passed away."

Not the sort of pressure I was imagining, then. I nod. I don't really remember Auntie Di but I know she was close with Grandma. They both stayed at the caravan together every summer before she died. I can just about picture her in my mind which means I must have come to visit Grandma at the caravan when I was younger. I wish I could remember more of that.

"Well, depending on the weather we can practice some more," Grandma says.

I'm not sure whether I want it to rain or clear up. I could do with more time to improve my bridge playing and understand how to bid without just guessing at numbers, but we've had almost a week since the weather was good enough to do anything other than hang out at the caravan or club house. While that's made it easy to avoid Autumn, a swim or afternoon on the beach would be a very nice change.

I finish my bacon sandwich. "What was the weather like on your power walk?" I ask, itching to use air quotes around power.

"A hint of sunshine, my dear. Maybe we can take the deck to the beach with us?" Grandma says, her mouth full of half chewed sliced white and bacon.

"Sounds great."

"Of course, we'll have to be back in time to change for the clubhouse show tonight. We can't miss that, can we?" Another rhetorical Grandma question.

"Whatever you say, Grandma." Anne nods in silent agreement. I hope Autumn won't be singing again tonight.

†

The day passes too quickly as the sun is around for more than just a fleeting visit. I'm enjoying the change of routine again, and I forget to worry about whether or not

To Autumn

Autumn will be at the clubhouse tonight. Grandma has lent me a book about bridge that she borrowed from Mr Hooper, which explains things a lot more clearly than she does, and the game starts to make a bit of sense in theory.

Dean's family joins us after lunch. I much prefer to hang out with him with everyone around as there's less chance he will try and sneak in a snog with me. We swim in the sea despite it not being all that warm today, and while we are treading water, he holds my hand. A wave comes and detangles us, and I take the chance to swim away knowing he can't catch me. It reminds me of the first time I swam in the sea here, instead then I was the person left watching someone swim away. No butterflies in my stomach today. Not about Dean, anyway.

We make plans with the Jacksons to see them up at the club house later before Grandma drags us back to the caravan to change and have dinner.

"Maybe we'll give your dad a call on our way over tonight," she says, and this perks up both Anne and me.

†

The phone booth has the usual queue of lone parents and kids waiting to make calls home to say they arrived safely and who are trying not to feel homesick. I can't believe how quickly I've become accustomed to everything here, the brand new environment and routine very different from what life is normally like. I don't feel as homesick as I did on those first few days. I'm sort of used to not seeing

Mum and Dad, or even speaking to Dad that often. I'm becoming an expert at reading Anne's silent communication. Even Grandma has become less annoying. Perhaps being here, away for the summer, isn't entirely a bad thing. It is nice not to have to worry about Mum every single day.

    I've brought my roll of silver coins with me, hoping to have more than the usual couple of minutes. When it's finally our turn, I pick up the handset and Grandma stands aside letting me dial, although she can't resist a look at her watch to remind us we're on a deadline. Dad picks up quickly. Almost straight away I realise there's not much to say as we've been stuck indoors mostly because of the weather.

    "I'm learning to play bridge," I say, mostly because there is literally nothing else to talk about.

    "Your gran's persuaded you, has she? I hope you're a better partner to her than I ever was. She becomes surprisingly competitive at the bridge table." He laughs at this. "And is Anne doing well?"

    Anne nods. "Yes, she's fine," I say. "She's nearly finished all the word searches though."

    "Right. Well maybe I can bring some down?" Dad says this like he can just pop down tomorrow.

    "That's a long way to come just to drop off some word search books."

    "Well…I was thinking I could come and visit. On your results day. I could pop to the school first thing and pick up the grade slips from Mrs Simpson and drive them down to you. That way you'll have them the same day as everyone else. I'm sure you're dying to see how well you've done."

Dad finishes and for once I wish we only had a ten pence length call cutting me off before I have to make a reply.

"I don't want to take you away from Mum if she needs you more…" I say, at a loss to think of an excuse for him not to come. I've been hoping that I might be able to delay the impending disaster of revealing how I've messed up those exams a little bit longer because I'm not at home.

"Don't be silly, Rob. She knows how hard you've worked for this. You deserve to celebrate your results."

Then the pips finally do start to click, and I have to scramble to reply before we're cut off. "I'm happy to wait until I'm home, really." The phone is dead before I finished my words. I hang up and Grandma twists her face.

"I wanted to have a word with your dad," she says.

"There's such a long queue now, Grandma, and I thought you wanted to go to the club house."

"I suppose so," she agrees, and we start to walk to the clubhouse.

"Dad was talking about coming to visit us. On results day, a week Thursday," I say, hoping to divert her sulk and find an ally in putting a stop to his plan. "Don't you think it might be too far to come just for one day? I can wait for my results."

"Don't be silly, darling, it will be lovely to see him. He could stay for a couple of nights. I'm sure he wants to visit you as well. He's not thinking only about exam results. He'll want to see you both. And I bet you'll want to know your grades as soon as they're out." Her tone closes off any change for a reply that contradicts what she has just said.

    Luckily, we arrive at the building and by the time we're through the doors and sitting down, the conversation is forgotten. Grandma hands me a fiver and waves me off to the bar. Mr Hooper hovers near our table while the band start their instrument warm up. As I wobble back trying to hold three glasses steady, I can hear Mr Hooper telling Grandma that the "delightful Australian lass" will be performing again. Perfect.

    As I'm handing out the drinks the Jacksons arrive. We all squish into the booth, and I'm stuck in the middle next to Dean, unable to escape. The lights go down and Mr Hooper steps up and starts his usual routine that I now know doesn't change very much from week to week. Within seconds, Autumn steps out and the band start playing an unusual arrangement of Kylie's "Confide in Me." There's a loud cheer followed by a whoop from the other side of the stage, and I recognise some of the holiday park staff gathered in a small group, along with some new faces.

    "This is for a good friend of mine," Autumn says, looking towards her mates, and then quickly towards our table, before she starts singing. She kills it. The band are barely noticeable behind her. Again, her group of friends cheers obnoxiously. Mr Hooper steps out to give thanks to Autumn and move things on. She clambers down off the

To Autumn

front of the stage and disappears into a huddle of lifeguards and waiters.

After some attempts at humour on stage, Mr Hooper announces a bar break. Autumn and her friends make a loud exit and then Mr Hooper joins our table.

"Hello, Robyn," he says. "Wasn't she wonderful again, your friend?" Dean coughs and then tries to stifle it.

"Sure," I reply. "As usual."

"I'm looking forward to our bridge match tomorrow evening. I think Autumn will make a delightful playing partner. We'll have a lovely time, young and old together." He chuckles.

I look to Grandma. She has not mentioned that Autumn will be the fourth person in our game.

"Yes. It'll be lovely," Grandma says, genuinely. I thought she would have understood that spending time with Autumn is not on my wish list at the moment. "A chance for you two to get to know each other a bit better."

Dean's hand slides over mine. "Sounds terrible," he whispers.

"Can't wait," I say. A familiar churning feeling returns to my stomach.

Chapter Thirteen

I've spent almost twenty-four hours trying to think of a way to dodge the impending bridge game. Faking flu, trying to convince Grandma my bridge skills aren't match ready, and suggesting that it won't be fair to Anne to exclude her, have all turned out to be unsuccessful rouses.

I haven't spoken to Autumn since she outed me and then caught me kissing Dean. Things couldn't be more awkward between us. What if she brings up the misunderstanding we had?

I load our dinner plates into the washing up bowl ready to take them down to the sinks. At least I can delay things with that.

To Autumn

"Hurry back," Grandma shouts as I leave. "They'll be here any minute." Great.

I walk as slow as I'm able, and when I reach the sinks, my stomach sinks a little more as I catch sight of the back of Dean's head at the middle sink. With a space next to him. I sidle up and turn the taps. He looks over.

"Hi!" he says, a grin forming.

"Alright." My glum mood shines bright.

"What's up? What did you do today?"

"Not much." I shrug.

"You okay?" he pushes. I need to say something, or he'll start to worry.

"Yeah, I'm just not looking forward much to the bridge evening tonight." This prompts a reminder that Autumn is going to be there.

"Oh right. With that lifeguard. Why don't you bail? Come over to ours instead?" Not exactly a better offer, spending all evening trying to avoid Dean's advances. What am I doing here?

"Thanks, but I can't. I promised Grandma and I don't want to let her down."

He has finished drying his plates and stacks them in his bowl.

"Night then," he says, and leans in to kiss me. I turn my head a little, and the kiss lands on my cheek. "See you tomorrow?" he asks, his voice a little quieter.

"Okay. Maybe at the pool," I reply and turn back to my sink. I should hurry up, or I will be in trouble.

†

As I walk up to the mobile home, the front door that leads into the living room is open. Mr Hooper and Autumn are inside, being shown to a seat at the dining table. They have chosen to sit opposite each other meaning I'm going to be sitting next to either Autumn or Mr Hooper.

I trip on the top step of the caravan entrance announcing my arrival with the clatter of crockery and cutlery. Grandma lets out a little yelp and comes over to fuss and panic about whether anything is broken. My face is fully flushed once again in the presence of Autumn.

"You certainly know how to make an entrance, Robyn," Autumn says, but without her usual sarcastic undertone.

"Nothing's broken. Let's put that down and start, shall we?" Grandma says. "Robyn, can you top up everyone's drinks please? There's a bottle of wine in the fridge. And a lemonade for you."

I do as I'm told. "Where's Anne?"

"She's watching a film with the Jacksons. Right, Mr Hooper, you shuffle and I'll deal," Grandma says and hands the deck over to him as she sits down next to him. Shit. She smooths out her notebook and lines up her pencil, marking out who is in charge for the evening. "Gosh, I haven't played a proper game of bridge since Di passed away. Excuse me if I'm rusty, that's over ten years ago. Do you play often,

Autumn? I know Mr Hooper does, he's been badgering me to play with him forever."

"I play competitively, Mrs Gale," Autumn says, her ambivalent humour coming across once more.

"Fantastic dear. Now in terms of partnering, I think it might be good for Robyn and I to separate as we are clearly not in the same league as you two experts." Gran laughs, and nudges Mr Hooper.

"How about the oldies against the youngsters?" Mr Hooper contributes.

"You're on," Autumn says. "Come on, Robyn, sit down. I won't bite."

Mr Hooper hands Grandma the shuffled deck and she starts to deal. Once we're all holding our cards, she smooths out the paper once more.

"Right, make your bids then." That's the last thing I fully understand as I spend most of the following two hours trying to keep up. Fortunately, Autumn is a bridge pro and coaches me as we go. Soon, we are starting to win some hands.

Grandma starts to yawn and as I'm dealing out, she says, "Shall we make this the last for the night?" We all nod.

Mr Hooper and Grandma dominate the final hand. "We must do this again!" Mr Hooper says enthusiastically. "You weren't rusty at all, Gloria." Grandma beams.

"I'd love to join again if you'll have me. With a bit more practice, Robyn will make an excellent partner,"

Autumn says, without a trace of sarcasm. "Maybe next time we can make it interesting? Put some stakes on the table?"

"What do you mean, dear?" Grandma asks.

"Ten pence a hand? Nothing to break the bank."

"I'll save up my shrapnel," says Mr Hooper.

Grandma and I step out of the booth to let everyone stand up. I have to move to the side so they can reach the door, but wherever I stand I'm in the way. Mr Hooper bends down and kisses Grandma on the cheek.

"See you soon, Gloria. Goodnight, girls." He leaves with a swoosh.

"I'm going to pick up Anne," Grandma says. "Goodnight Autumn." She leaves and shuts the door behind her. The cool air hangs between Autumn and me.

"Well…" I say, but not able to find any words to follow.

"I had a fun time, Robyn," Autumn says, pulling on a hoodie. "I'm glad I said yes. I wasn't sure you'd want to see me."

All the things I want to say back: I wasn't sure either; I've felt sick all day but now I'm floating on air; my goosebumps aren't from the cold; I've played the mixtape every night while I'm falling asleep; I can't stop thinking about you.

"I hope you find your voice again soon, Robyn," Autumn says as she opens the door.

"Night," I croak to her back as she skips down the stairs.

To Autumn

Chapter Fourteen

Results day. The end of my world looms. We have to wait for Dad to drive the five hours it takes to reach here, giving me a short stay of execution. Grandma wakes us up early to help her do a "top to bottom" clean of the mobile home before Dad arrives. This is how I am going to spend my final hours alive, scrubbing a caravan toilet.

Dean knocks on the door at about 11 o'clock, excited.

"Six As and three Bs," he says, instead of hello. "How did you do?"

"Dad's not here yet. He promised not to open the envelope before he gets here."

"I thought your dad was working abroad?" Dean asks but luckily Grandma cuts him off.

"Are your parents taking you out to celebrate, Dean?" Grandma says. "Maybe we could all have dinner together? As a double celebration."

"Yes! I mean, if Robyn wants to," Dean and Grandma's enthusiasm makes the concrete block in my stomach swell.

"Of course she does. You'll be able to meet her dad."

A done deal. Well until the truth about my exam failure comes out. I do my best to smile.

"Come and find us later at the beach," Dean says and bounces out of the mobile home.

"No doubt we'll be boasting nine A stars in a few hours, Robyn!" Grandma shouts to his back, not hiding her pride at the thought.

"What if…" I start but am unable to find the words I want to say.

"Yes, dear?"

What if I've messed everything up and you all disown me?

"Nothing." I go back to cleaning the bathroom.

†

I pound the lengths of the pool, trying to push down my worry about the impending disaster. I have feelings of guilt so strong that I wish Dad wasn't driving all the way down here, even though I really want to see him and know he wants to see Anne and me, and I'm trying to avoid Autumn's gaze as she is on duty today and thinks we are friends again since we played bridge together. What a mess. Which all originates with me giving into my stupid fantasy that it's okay for me to be gay. If I hadn't kissed Beth, then Mum wouldn't have attempted suicide, and I wouldn't have messed up my exams, and I wouldn't have met Autumn. Life would just be carrying on as normal, and we'd all be happy. It really is all my fault.

 I pick at the cheese and tomato sandwiches Grandma made us for lunch. I can't taste anything, and my stomach is again full with the huge block of concrete that has made a home there.

 "Nervous about seeing your dad?" Grandma asks, as if she's solved a difficult crossword puzzle.

 "I'm just anxious to see him, that's all."

 Anne is stuffing her face and takes the remains of bread and cheese from my plate and has that for herself, too. I clear the table and rinse the empty plates at the sink – Grandma has made an allowance for low-mess meals, and now we don't have to drag everything down to the central sinks after every single meal.

 "What time did Dad say he was leaving home?" I ask, checking the clock again. The second hand is spinning by, eager to speed up his arrival.

 "He wanted to be on the road for seven this morning, that was the earliest he could arrive at the school to pick up your results. I expect he'll be here very soon unless there's been an accident on the A303."

 "Right."

"We'll know when he gets here!" Grandma says as though she has made the funniest of jokes.

†

Not even reading Keats calms me today. And then, there's the sound of a familiar shoe hitting the ground. Without looking I know Dad has arrived. His aftershave floats in the caravan ahead of him.

"Hello? Anybody here?" he calls as he steps inside. No sign of the results envelope. I stand up, unsure whether to cry or hug him. Instead, I do nothing, then a thundering of footsteps as Anne crashes through the entrance and leaps onto him.

"Dad!" she shouts, muffled through Dad's Hawaiian shirt.

I'm still frozen until Dad says to me, "Come here muffin, you're not too old to give your dad a hug, even if you are sixteen now."

Grass lump in my throat, concrete in my stomach, I step towards them and join the jumble of arms and snotty noses. I bury my head into Dad's shoulder, willing the tears to retreat back into my eyeballs. After a long minute, when none of us can breathe any longer, we pull apart. Dad gives us a standard once up and down, the way all relatives do when they haven't seen younger relatives for a while.

"You've both grown! And such suntans. I barely recognise you." Dad looks just the same, and I am very

To Autumn

happy about that. I don't think I could handle any more change right now. "Okay, presents!"

"Yes!" Anne says. And I realise what seems wrong with this picture, well aside from the Hawaiian shirt. Anne is speaking! When did that start?

Grandma, who has been quietly waiting at the door, steps in. She kisses Dad on the cheek, leaving her mark of bright red lips of course, and offers Dad a cup of tea.

"Put the kettle on, Robyn, dear," she says when Dad nods.

Glad of something to do and a further delay to the results disaster coming to light, I fill the kettle and pull out a tea pot. Dad opens the holdall that was slung over his shoulder.

"Right, Anne, for you…some new puzzle books. I hear you've become quite the expert."

"She has," Grandma agrees, even though she must have been the one who told Dad.

"Thank you," Anne says as she rips open the wrapping paper.

Why had no one else noticed that Anne is speaking again? Am I supposed to pretend this is completely normal and not mention it?

I bang the cups as I pull them out of the cupboard. I feel too sick to make a tea for myself as well. My hands are shaking.

"And, darling, I haven't forgot you," Dad says in my direction. "But first, we must celebrate your exam success."

I wish I could run away right now. I know I've failed them all. I'm not going to be able to go to college. I'm going to end up somewhere washing dishes forever. If they'd even take me.

I bring the teas over to the sofa and then Dad hands me an envelope. I stare at it, knowing my future plans of English A Levels and then an English Literature degree at Warwick or Durham will be shattered the second I open it. Knowing I'll have let down everyone, Dad, Mum, my school, me, and that there's no more hiding from it.

"There's something I need to tell you…" I start, looking at Dad.

"Hurry up, dear," Grandma says, "we've waited all morning for this!"

I tear the envelope slowly, revealing three dot matrix print outs. The first tells me exactly what I expected, French and Double Science: E grades. The next tells me, History and Geography Ds – saved a little by coursework submitted last year – then Maths and Classics, also Es. English Language and Lit to go. Taking in a deep breath, I turn to the last sheet. A shiver runs through me. Somehow, I didn't fuck up everything. There in black and white, it says English Language: B, English Literature A. How I managed this, I couldn't explain.

Three sets of eyes peer at me, waiting for me to share the news.

"I think you'd better sit down," I say, trying to make a joke as they are all already sitting down. "I did about as well as I expected… the grades I deserve, I think. Except for English, I didn't deserve those results." I hand the papers over to Dad. His smile flattens as he takes in the fact that I'm a big old failure.

"Oh, honey. I should have realised. I should have asked the school to let you defer."

"I've ruined your visit."

"No!" Dad says and leans over for a hug. Our tears flow into each other's. "I'm the parent. I didn't even ask you if you needed help with schoolwork. I just assumed because you went there every day you were fine."

"I couldn't concentrate at all," I confess. "All I could think about was Mum…" and how what happened to her was my fault. "I've ruined my chances of going to college and uni!"

We pull apart and another voice I'd been dreading to hear from speaks up. "Robyn, dear, believe it or not O Level results don't make or break a person."

"GCSEs," I say.

"Well, GSCEs then. Let's have a look and see if anything can be salvaged here." Dad hands Grandma the slips of paper. She smiles. "Robyn, look how well you did in English!" I know, but I also know they should have both been A* grades.

"I did okay in those subjects." Anne hands me a new tissue, one that isn't snot dissolved, and sits down next to me.

"Better than okay," Dad chips on. "Really, really well. I'm proud of you." I give him a look that questions the validity of his statement. "I am. You've both been through some very tough circumstances this year, and frankly, it's a miracle you're coping as well as you are. I haven't been able to give you what you needed, that's one of the reasons I thought it would be good for you to be here, with Mum."

"And it has been good for them, John. Anne and I have lovely conversations even though I know she finds that hard, and Robyn has made some wonderful friends." Right. "Robyn, what is it you wanted to do next, after you finished school?"

I pause. What is it I want? I am tempted to tell them that all I really want to do is watch *Neighbours* with Autumn every day, but I know that's not a suitable answer, and I know that could never happen, anyway.

"Just go to college, with my friends, do English and other A-Levels I guess, and then maybe go to university to do English as well. But you need at least a C in the core subjects to do that, and Bs or higher to go to a good uni." I'm parroting what our Head of Year has been telling us for the last two years.

To finally say all of this out loud is a huge relief compared to months of keeping it buried deep inside. The worst has happened. Well, the worst happened four months ago. It didn't occur to me to think that rubbish GCSE results are nothing in comparison to your mum trying to kill herself. It didn't occur to me that people might understand that it

To Autumn

would be hard for me to focus on revising and exam questions given everything else going on. I just thought I had to keep acting like nothing had happened, because that's what everyone else was doing.

Dad doesn't say anything. "But… you won't be disappointed if I don't go to a good uni?"

Grandma pipes up, "Robyn, I'll make sure you end up at whatever university you choose, don't you worry, dear."

I laugh. "How? You can't bribe UCAS."

"No. But you're willing to do the work, and where there's a will, there's a way. That's what Di used to say, and she was right. You'll do retakes, you'll cover the ground you needed, and if it takes a bit longer, then so be it. There's no deadline on achieving your dreams."

Where has this person come from and what have they done with Grandma?

"I feel awful. You came all this way to see us, Dad, and to celebrate, and there's nothing to celebrate now." I start crying again.

"Actually, there is. I have some news to share with you both." He pats Anne on the head. "I can't believe no one else has mentioned it, but Anne seems to have found her voice again. That's two things. Plus an A in English. Three things."

The concrete block in my stomach shrinks a little, and all the muscles I've been clenching start to relax of their own accord. Who would have thought that everyone finding out about my disaster would be the very thing to stop me having to worry about it? Too bad I can't tell them about why Mum really drove herself into the hospital wall.

To Autumn

CHAPTER FIFTEEN

We have a table booked for dinner, as a treat, and as we arrive, I can see a few tables are also celebrating exam results. Dean's family are here too, and Grandma asks the blond Leo-alike waiter to seat us on the table next to them. My appetite completely disappears as this means not only will I have to introduce Dean to Dad, but I will also have to come clean to Dean and his family about how badly I did in my exams.

The Jacksons wave hello and Grandma steps in to do the introductions. Dean's quizzical look reminds me I need to explain why Dad is here now and not working abroad. He stands up to shake Dad's hand though and then winks at me when he thinks no one else is looking.

We sit down and I hide behind my menu. Dean drags his chair over next to me.

"So…how'd the genius do, then?" he asks, as though he thinks the reason I haven't made a big deal about my results is because I'm embarrassed about how well I've done.

"Pretty much as I thought," I say, keeping it vague.

"Wow, ten A stars then, I'm gonna guess."

"Something like that…"

"Dean, leave the poor girl alone, will you? I'm sure she just wants to catch up with her dad and celebrate with her family," Mrs Jackson says, and Dean reluctantly turns his chair back around to his own table.

"Robyn and Dean have spent a lot of time together this summer," Grandma tells Dad, with a knowing smile.

"Is that so? Well, I'm glad coming to stay here hasn't been all bad," Dad says, trying to hide a smile.

"Yes, but she has another friend too. Autumn. She's a lifeguard and she's Australian!" Anne chips in.

I'd be glad if the ground swallowed me up right about now.

"Dad, didn't you say you had some news to tell us?" I'm desperate to move the conversation away from my fake boyfriend and my complicated secret crush.

"Yes, of course. Let's order and then we can talk. I can't believe the menu is almost the same as when I used to come here when I was your age, Robyn."

"When did you come here, Dad?" Anne asks, and I appreciate the distraction.

To Autumn

"I've been bringing your dad here for decades," Grandma joins in, "since he was your age Anne, maybe even before. I didn't always have my own mobile home, though; we used to have to hire ours along with the other weekly visitors. Di and I bought the mobile home we're in now a few years before Robyn was born. Robyn won't remember it, but your mum and dad brought her here when she was a baby. And of course, she stayed here for a while when Anne was born."

This is news to me, but I can't concentrate on that for now. There are too many other things on my mind. How will I sort out my GCSE results? What news does Dad have? And how can I ask Dad to let Mum know I have a sort of boyfriend?

"Speaking of Mum," Dad seizes the chance to speak again, "that's what my news is related to." My blood runs cold then quickly heats again as it rises up my cheeks. She's told Dad why she drove into the wall, I'm sure of it. Anne takes my hand. I sneak a look Dean's way, and the Jacksons are deep in family banter, not paying any attention to us.

"Your mum is…doing much, much better. I didn't want to say anything until we knew for sure, but her new treatment seems to be working. I can see her old self coming back." More tears. Will I have any left by the end of the day? "I told you we had something to celebrate." He smiles and puts his arm around me.

"What sort of treatment?" I say, picking up that he has been a bit vague on the details.

"Well, they used a special treatment which isn't used very often, you see. And it sounds scarier than it really is, but without the medication working properly we didn't have many options left. Your mum's had several courses of EST – electric shock therapy." A picture of Mum hooked up to some kind of giant cackling machine as Dr Frankenstein charges her with lightning strength electricity burns its way into my mind.

Grandma doesn't look surprised. "It sounds worse than it actually is. From what your dad explained to me, they make your mum very relaxed, she's not conscious during the process, and can't feel anything. Then they send gentle currents to her brain to help it reset to the right levels of chemicals. She doesn't feel any pain at all." What Grandma doesn't know though, is that this is all my fault. I've put Mum on a bed where electricity is being sent to her brain.

Leo the waiter arrives to take our order. None of us have even looked at the menu and Grandma sends him away again.

"This was meant to be good news!" Dad says, sensing mine and Anne's surprise. "I didn't finish. The thing is, the treatment's working. Whatever is happening in her mind, she's coming back. She's tired, and it affects her memory, but we're finally talking to the doctors about her coming home!"

Leo comes back to take our order, but I can't be here anymore. Before he opens his mouth, I stand up and leave the table. Dad calls after me, but I keep walking.

To Autumn

At the toilets, I crash into someone coming out of the men's. Dean. He smiles but I don't smile back.

"What's going on?" he says, thinking that he has a right to know.

"I need to get out of here."

"Come with me, then," Dean says, and takes my hand, pulling me towards the exit.

It's easier just to take his lead. I follow Dean out to the vestibule area, wanting to avoid a spectacle if that's possible. Since Dad arrived, everything has gone to pot. I have spent every day since we arrived here building up a scenario that was working for me, and more importantly, that could help Mum. Today was supposed to be a chance to show Dad, and then when he goes home, he can tell Mum and it will help her recovery. Then, maybe, when we go home in a few weeks, things can return to normal.

"What's wrong?" he asks. "Has something happened? Is that why your dad has come back to England?"

"Erm, no. Not really. He just wanted to see us. Bring me my GCSE results"

"But not your Mum?" Dean continues, looking very confused as his brow creases into his nose.

I don't want to start unravelling this conversation right now.

"No… she was tied up in work stuff."

"I thought it was your dad who was working abroad?" Why the interrogation?

"They both were. Anyway, that's not important right now." I am desperate to change the subject, but then I don't want to give away the real reason I am not acting myself. Learning about the electric treatment. Seeing Autumn like that, with Leo, and then dedicating that song to her "friend." I didn't expect something like that to upset me this much. Almost as much as the day Mum…

"Well, what's so important, that it's put you in this strange mood?" Dean pulls me towards the wall as holidaymakers pass through entering and exiting the club house.

"I'm not in a mood," I say, in a voice that is not going to convince anyone.

"Time of the month?"

This makes me want to hit him.

"Why do boys think anytime a girl is upset it must be to do with PMT?" I ask, nearly shouting. Where do they learn that from?

"Well, once a month we have to pretend my mum doesn't have PMT either," he replies, as if that's an okay thing to say.

"I don't have PMT. It's nothing. I'm fine." No one would believe me.

"Well, if it isn't PMT, then maybe we can go somewhere, and I can help you forget about whatever it is you're not upset about. We've been going out for nearly three weeks."

To Autumn

The conversation I've really been hoping won't take place is starting. How have I gone from one undesirable question to another in the space of seconds? How do I steer this in another direction?

Dean moves towards me, but I pull back.

"I don't think now's the right time for that. You were right. There is something. My head is all over the place. But I'm sorry I don't want to talk about it."

"I wasn't suggesting we talk," Dean says and tries on a smile that I think is supposed to be an attempt at seduction.

My patience is wearing very thin, and we've been gone long enough for Grandma and Dad to notice by now. I'm sure they'll be coming round the corner any second.

"No!" I say, my voice loud, echoing in the hallway. And that's when I see Autumn. She is the person coming round the corner.

"What's going on?" she asks, in her stern lifeguard voice, stepping up her pace to reach us.

"None of your business," Dean says, not looking her or me in the face. His dislike of Autumn is more evident than ever.

"I saw you run out of the dining room, Robyn," she says, I hadn't even realised she was in there. She must have been visiting Leo. "I said to your dad and Mrs Gale that I'd come and find you. They were worried." She talks directly to me, ignoring Dean. "Are you okay? Do you need any help?"

"I'm fine. Why does everyone keep asking that? There's nothing wrong with me." I try to assert just how fine

I want to seem, despite how not fine I'm feeling. Explaining this to Autumn might even be worse than fobbing off Dad and Grandma.

"She doesn't need your help," Dean says, finally addressing Autumn directly. "We were just leaving, right Robyn?" He takes my elbow but instinctively I pull it away from his grip. His face flickers, and he looks like a wounded puppy. An elderly couple in matching velure tracksuits enter and give the three of us a disapproving look.

"I need to get out of here," I say, and in the same movement turn and make a dash for the door before it swings shut.

To Autumn

CHAPTER SIXTEEN

I keep running, not really paying attention to where I am heading, keen to leave behind Autumn and Dean and Dad.

Three weeks since arriving at the holiday park and the nights are already drawing in much earlier. Solar-powered miniature streetlamps light the pathways around the park. In the dark it can be even harder to navigate the maze of caravans. Although I am looking for a place where no one will find me, I'm running through rows of homes that I don't recognise. Families are sitting at their dining tables playing card games or watching their portable televisions. I wish I could invite myself in to join them and escape this situation I have created for myself.

Finally, I find my bearings, as my breath is starting to expire, and soon enough I'm able to go towards the playground, returning to the scene of a recent crime – leading Dean on.

I know now where I want to be. I slow to a walk past the gang drinking their warm cider, the fug of their cigarette smoke even more ethereal in the belated twilight. I try and catch my breath.

I head straight to the nature reserve, not stopping for small talk, hoping for calm and solitude inside. My bench awaits my arrival.

I sit, but before I even have time to put my head in my hands, there's a sound of leaves rustling and a twig snapping under someone's indiscrete step.

"Robyn." Autumn.

I didn't think anyone would come after me, given the exit I made.

"You found me." My voice is steel, I'm done with pleasantries.

"I knew you'd come here." She knows me better than myself.

"Are you sure your boyfriend isn't going to mind you came chasing after me?" I spit the words out.

"My boyfriend…? You're the one with the boyfriend. Robyn, I think you and I need to have a proper conversation. Lay some cards on the table."

"I've played more than enough cards over the last three weeks, thank you." I know she doesn't mean it literally, but I can't help the snipe. I'm shaking. What does she want to talk about? Is she referring to the mix tape? I feel inside my jacket pocket, my latest hiding place, and clutch the cassette box in my fingers.

"Tough crowd. Look, Robyn, I am sorry if I misunderstood about you and Dean. It just looked like he was trying to pressure you into something, and I wanted to make sure you were okay."

"He's my boyfriend, as you say, and he wasn't trying to force me to do anything." He was only following the lead I'd given him after all, but taking things further with Dean is about as far from what I want as sitting here having this humiliating conversation.

"Okay then. That's all I wanted to know." Autumn sits back as she says this.

"Why?" Instead of leaving it there and walking away, I'm determined to pick the scab of this awkward wound.

"Because. Because I care about you and don't want to see you hurt."

"You don't even know me. We watched a couple of episodes of *Neighbours* together and you think you care about me?" I don't know why I'm set on trying to hurt her.

"You remind me of me. The me who I was before I came to England."

Definitely not the answer I'm expecting from her. "What? You made your mum try to kill herself by kissing another girl, did you?" The words fly out before I have a chance to put a brake on them. Probably not the answer she expected back, either. I know how to kill a conversation.

She leans against the bench's backrest and closes her eyes. An age of a few seconds passes. We've hit the speed of light on confessions.

Autumn opens her eyes, and turns to face me, making sure I'm looking at her. She catches my gaze.

"Not exactly, but close. Why do you think I would come all the way to freezing cold England for uni? I needed to be as far away as possible from my family. Because I'm a lesbian, and they didn't like the idea at first."

I'm stunned into silence, finally. No words spill uncontrollably out of my mouth, instead it opens and closes without noise.

We turn away from each other and lean back against the bench, both of us breathing deeply, like we've just finished running the most important race of our lives. Our thighs are touching, and I realise there's barely a hairline gap between us.

"Leo isn't your boyfriend then?" eventually forces its way out, between inhales and exhales.

"Leo? Oh, Bradley. No… he's in the family as well." I look confused. "Gay, I mean," she explains.

"He is? But his hands are always all over you."

"Friends are allowed to touch each other you know. We're at uni together. So, is he what all this has been about?"

"Amongst other things," I remind her. "Mostly my Mum. After she…went to hospital, I promised myself I'd find a boyfriend so that she'd not have to worry about me and might start to recover. Then tonight, Dad told us she's been having electric shock therapy and that the whole situation is my fault."

"So, your folks aren't working abroad. I did think it was strange for your dad to just show up like that today." She really has been paying attention. I can feel her eyes on me again, but she quickly turns her head away.

"No. He was looking after Mum while she's been in hospital. I don't really talk about it. No one outside the family knows."

"That's a big secret to carry all to yourself. That, and… you know." Autumn's shoulder bumps mine.

"I'm just one huge ball of secrets it seems. I…I've messed up my GCSEs too. The results came today. I failed almost everything. Except for English." No reason to keep any of the secrets inside anymore. The floodgate is open. I suddenly feel a lot lighter. Like I could float up into the night sky.

"Oh Robyn." Autumn looks at me in a way I don't quite understand. I look back at her, not sure how to feel about our sudden intimacy. "That's a lot. A lot to deal with."

Especially for someone my age, right? But those words don't follow her observation. She's still looking at me and I feel like I should be doing something more than staring gormlessly back into her eyes. Her words are going round and round my head. Have I really just told her everything that I've been trying to push down for the last four months? What is it about her that made me spill my guts without even thinking about it? And then, the bit where she said "I'm a lesbian" replays too. I was too busy talking about my own stuff that I almost missed Autumn telling me her stuff. Maybe I misheard her.

After what must be an unusually long silence, neither of us has spoken for several minutes now, I open my mouth. I'm about to ask her if she is a lesbian, if I really heard those words come out of her mouth, while her eyes are sinking deep into my soul. She adjusts herself and her fingers are gently grazing my arm. The stillness of the night is palpable, and my heart is beating loud enough to sound like the intro of a soft rock ballad.

My instinct is telling me to seize the fucking moment, and before I have a chance to question anything anymore, I lean in. Our lips are millimetres apart; her face close-up and disjointed like a surrealist portrait. She smells of peach. And coconut, always coconut.

She doesn't pull back. Her fingers twitch against the skin of my arm. I close my eyes and make the smallest of movements until our lips meet. The softness overwhelms me and draws me in further, and my tongue traces the gap, finding hers. A thunderbolt dances down my spine. Her hand takes a firmer grip and pulls my body closer. Her lips open a little and our tongues dance a waltz. There is nothing else in the world right now.

The soft rock ballad plays through, Autumn's heartbeat harmonising with mine. My lips smile into the kiss.

To Autumn

Then, a noise. A disturbance in the leaves. I pull back quickly, too quickly. The shock of my actions sinking in. I kissed Autumn. I kissed a woman, again. I broke my promise.

Autumn leans forward and tries to steer my face back to hers. Another rustle, then a cough. Someone is here. I turn my head and Dean is there, a few metres away, watching us, covered in sweat and playground dust. Autumn's head turns and she clocks the intruder.

"Shit," she breathes.

"What the fuck is going on, Robyn? Is she bothering you?"

"I don't think so, buddy," Autumn says before I have a chance to answer.

"I bet your girlfriend would say differently."

"I bet yours would, too."

What is going on here? My brain and mouth finally switch into gear.

"Dean! This isn't what it looks like." Not that I know what it looks like. "Please don't say anything, please. My parents can't know. I'm sorry."

"You will be." Dean turns around and runs. I stand up, thinking I should go after him, check he is okay, and try and talk him out of telling anyone. My life is over if he does.

I run his words over and stop at something I missed the significance of first time round.

"Wait. Your girlfriend?"

Autumn grimaces. "Robyn, I'm sorry. I was going to tell you. Right before you kissed me and I stopped being able to think. That was magic, right, it wasn't just me? I've never felt anything like that before."

"Stop. You have a girlfriend? Why would you do that? Why would you let that kiss happen if you have a girlfriend? He's lying, right? He's trying to mess with my head." I sway with dizziness, not able to make sense of what has happened in the last five minutes. This is exactly why I wanted to pretend none of these feelings were real. Everything becomes complicated, and I've just made it all worse. What if Dean is on his way to tell Dad and Grandma? I need to stop him.

I turn and take a step towards the direction he headed, back towards the club house.

"Robyn, wait. Please. Hayley is my girlfriend, yes. She's visiting this week. But I was going to end it before she went back home, I promise."

"Why?"

"Because. It doesn't feel right anymore. Not since–"

"I meant, why did you lie to me? Why didn't you tell me?" My heart's pounding like a heavy metal gig now.

Autumn doesn't say anything. She stands there. Looking at me. I'm a mug. Why didn't I just keep my cool? Keep it all inside. She tricked me into trusting her. I won't give her a chance to lie anymore. I'm gone before she can say anything else to hurt me.

To Autumn

Chapter Seventeen

"Did your friend find you, love?" Dad asks as I skulk back into the mobile home. I thought they'd still be eating dinner. "We decided to have a takeaway instead of eating at the restaurant. There's spag bol for you if you'd like it? I know that's your favourite."

Grandma and Anne are eating at the table. My appetite's well and truly lost.

"I just want to go to bed," I sigh. Even though what I really want, more than anything right now, is a hug from Mum. The one thing I can't have.

"If that's what you need, then… okay. We can talk tomorrow before I go home. Today was a big day, and I'm sorry you're having to deal with everything at once, darling."

He has no idea. He walks over and kisses my forehead, and then I turn into my room. I'm grateful for the cave-like space of the bunk bed. Finally, I feel warm and safe. Not having to talk to anyone or perform as the Robyn they expect means the millions of thoughts in my head have some time to move about, and they play as if I've unpressed pause. I have both a sense of relief and terror giving these thoughts a chance to be heard rather than constantly trying to push them away.

Despite the jumble of noise in my head, my mind starts to settle pretty quickly. I replay the day and try to understand what's happened.

One: Dad came to visit. It was more emotional than I expected after not seeing him for over three weeks.

Two: Exam results. My worst fears about how badly I'd fucked up came true. But no one shouted at me, I'm still alive, and perhaps bad results won't be the end of the world I expected. Maybe there's a bigger future than working as a dishwasher for the rest of my life.

Three: Dean. Not just Dean. Me and Dean. I've let this become complicated because I was trying to use him to make my life easier. That isn't fair. But then, neither is his threat to me. I know he must be hurt and confused. As am I. Is he my boyfriend? Is that something I want to keep pretending at? What if he tells Grandma or someone about seeing me kiss Autumn. How can I stop him doing that? What a mess.

Four: Mum. Another situation that's my fault. All of my problems keep coming back to me kissing Beth. What if she tells Dad and they all know I'm really the one to blame?

To Autumn

What if she never wants to see me again because I remind her of what happened? I don't think pretending to have a boyfriend is the answer to that. Well, not Dean as my boyfriend anyway. Perhaps I'll just be celibate. I could become a nun. Maybe. They don't have complicated love lives. Do they? No. They're not allowed. Something to consider. I probably won't need GCSE results either. But I probably need to believe in God and go to church which makes that a bit tricky.

    Five: Autumn. Where do I start? She did think I'm a lesbian. Well, she's also right. How did she know? I mean, could she tell just by looking at me? Did she know because she is too? That's the least of my worries at the moment. I don't think she'll tell anyone I kissed her. But Dean might. How do I stop him? How do I apologise to him? I kissed her! It was incredible. Better than I've imagined. I think she wanted it too…she didn't pull away. But what about her girlfriend? This Hayley? Why didn't Autumn tell me she has a girlfriend before? She's been lying to me as much as I've been lying to everyone else. That's some karma for me, I suppose. Probably better if I just stay away from Autumn. That will definitely make a lot of the other situations easier. And I need to focus on sorting out college or doing exam retakes or something. Not that I can cope with repeating a year at school.

    What do I do? I need a plan. If I actually do something, maybe I'll be able to stop worrying and thinking about it all.

Chapter Eighteen

Somewhere amongst all of those thoughts, I drifted into a deep sleep and didn't even dream. I think I was exhausted, not physically, but emotionally. My head feels lighter this morning, and the concrete block in my stomach seems to have shrunk. I'm starving. I didn't eat anything at all last night.

Despite everything that's been going on, it feels good that some of the secrets I've been keeping are now released. There's more space for the remaining one I still want to keep for now, at least while Mum's starting to get better.

Perhaps there's still a chance I can go to college with my friends after all. I just have to figure out how to make it happen. And now I know Autumn has a girlfriend, there's no reason for us to continue to be friends. I don't need her. And Dean, well that might need some work to sort out. On the one hand, I don't think I'll need to worry about him trying to kiss me again. On the other, he might tell someone what he saw and then I'll have a lot to answer for. We're only here for two and a bit more weeks. I hope I can hang in for that long.

The smell of bacon wafts into our room. I wonder who's cooking, as that has become my job. Anne's soft snores from the top bunk tell me she doesn't have anything to do with it. I have to make time to speak to her today and find out when she started talking again and how that happened. How did I miss that?

I shrug on my dressing gown and open our door as quietly as possible, trying not to wake Anne. Dad is stealthily moving around the kitchen, his hands full of mugs, ketchup, and milk. I whisper good morning and grab the breakfast things from him. He kisses the top of my head again, such a Dad-thing to do, then places half of the bacon back in the oven.

We sit down, facing each other at the table, as the settee is still covered in bedsheets.

"Your gran filled me in on some things," Dad says, before taking a bite of his bacon sarnie. I put down the half sandwich I am about to stuff into my mouth.

"Grandma," I say on reflex. "I mean, like what?" I ask, trying to sound casual.

"Your sandwich'll get cold," Dad replies. I take a bite.

"Well, for one thing, it seems Anne's been chatting away to her for most of the summer. You really didn't know?"

I shake my head. My mind has been in too many other places rather than being present. I've barely noticed what's been right in front of me.

"I'm over the moon. Your mum will be too. Another motivation for her to work on her recovery." He pauses and takes another mouthful of sandwich and a swig of tea. I keep eating so I don't have to say anything.

"Your gran – grandma, also said that Dean might be your boyfriend?" I extend my chewing. "Which is fine, of course. He seems nice." I've run out of sandwich.

"I guess he was sort of, for a minute. Not anymore though." I really hope this is enough information for Dad. And Mum.

"Did something happen?" Dad asks, suddenly very serious.

"No, we just…we just have different perspectives on a few things. And I want to focus on sorting out doing my resits and going to college. Will Mum be angry with me?"

"Your mum is very proud of you. Of you both. She just wants you to be happy and safe." Dad plays with his kitchen roll napkin. He sounds like he has more to say, but he stops there.

"I know," I reply, which might be the biggest lie I've ever told. Is that what Mum really wants?

A door banging open announces Grandma.

To Autumn

"Morning, everyone," she says bright and breezily. "I thought I'd wake up early to make the most of a day with John before he has to drive back to London. I'm really enjoying having all three of you here. It reminds me of old times, when this mobile home was packed full of family squeezed in here, there, and everywhere."

Then Anne follows. We squash into the booth while Dad tops up the tea and produces bacon sandwiches for Grandma and Anne.

"So," he says, still overcompensating with excitement, "what's the plan for today?"

Anything but the beach or the pool, please, anything to reduce the chances of bumping into Dean or Autumn.

"How about a change of scenery? A drive to Dartmoor and a nice, long walk? Perfect weather for it, sun behind a cloud."

"Yes, sounds good to me!" I say before Anne or Grandma have a chance to stop the plan.

"We'll take a picnic with us!" Dad says, again with a level of excitement that is too high for a walk on some slightly rocky low hills. "I'll do the washing up while you all shower and dress."

"Sure," I reply casually, hiding how much I appreciate another missed chance to bump into Dean. I wonder if he's told anyone what he saw yet. The news is probably all over the park by now. Just as well we are going offsite for the day. Maybe Dad'll let me go back home with him? If Mum's feeling better then there's no need for us to say here, is there? I have all day to drop the hint.

After we've all washed and dressed, I help Dad put some packed lunches together. His sandwich-making skills are no better than when we left, but he hasn't been practising, I suppose.

We walk to the car, and I keep my cap on and my head down. I can't avoid them seeing me because no doubt they'll notice Dad, Anne, and Grandma, but I can avoid seeing them.

†

"Remember when you, Di, and I used to come here, Mum?" Dad asks.

All of his happiest childhood memories include Aunt Di. Grandma spent a lot of time with her after Dad's father passed away when Dad was very little.

"Why have I waited so long to come back here?" he asks, though I don't think he's expecting an answer.

The unending view of rolling green-topped hills underneath an equally infinite off-white sky is one of the most beautiful things I've ever seen. The anticipation of trekking up and down into the horizon and leaving everything else behind feels like the first time anything has made sense in a long while. I won't even be alone with my thoughts, as the landscape has swallowed up all the darkness in my mind and painted over it in a countryside hue instead.

To Autumn

We're in a spot off the beaten track, which means we're not overcrowded with tourists. We consult the map and choose a direction, roughly westwards, to start off. After about five seconds, Grandma – donned in her power walking tracksuit no less – decides she is going to keep guard of the car instead.

"I'll be fine here with the deckchair and a book," she says, without the slightest concern that her moves might look planned.

"Sure thing, Mum," Dad says genially. "The girls and I will make do on our own."

We set off again, stretching our legs towards the great beyond. A comfortable silence settles between us and every now and then Dad breaks into a cheery off-tune whistle.

"This is what I'd do every day if we didn't have to work or go to school," Dad says.

"Me too!" Anne agrees.

I'm still not used to the sound of her voice being back. I nod along with them. I wonder why we haven't spent other summers down here then, if Dad loves it that much. He nods hello at an approaching dog walker, definitely a local as he's wearing a jumper and doesn't have a huge backpack to carry.

"We don't have that back home, do we?" Dad observes. It sounds as though he's trying to plant a seed for moving here.

"Why didn't you and Mum bring us here then?" I counter.

"We used to bring you all the time, Rob."

"I don't remember that."

"Well, mostly it was before Anne was born. Then we sort of stopped coming down. And then we got used to not coming here. It was too easy to fall into that trap of feeling like there's not enough time to do all the important things and instead spend a moment just watching life whizz by from the sidelines," Dad says.

I've never heard him talk like this before.

"I feel like if I don't sort out everything for college now, it'll be too late and I'll have ruined the rest of my life." The words come out before I even realise what I am saying.

"You do have plenty of time, believe it or not, and we'll make sure we find a way for you to make up your results. You have a bright future, Robyn, and you deserve our support. You too, Anne," he says, taking her hand.

"Thank you." I feel guilty. I doubt he would be this generous if he knew what I'd done with Beth and Autumn.

"If Mum's better, can we come home?" I ask, taking my chance with all the honesty and confessions going on.

"I want to stay here!" Anne says. Her forthrightness is a shock. "I love it here. We're having a proper holiday, and Grandma is awesome."

"I'm glad you like it, baby," Dad replies. "Rob, your Mum is getting better, but I think she still needs to focus on being ready to come home, and ease back into normal life. She's not going to be her old self straight away." Maybe

Mum did tell Dad, and now they don't really want me to come home at all.

"We're going to come and visit you though, on the last weekend of the holidays. If all things go well, Mum and I will drive down, stay for two nights, and then we can all go home together. What do you think?"

"Can you tape *Neighbours* for me? There's nowhere to watch it here." I'll keep trying to persuade him, one way or another.

"I thought your gran said that you'd found a friend who watches it?"

"That… didn't work out." I don't want to be probed on that further. "I can give you instructions on how to set the VCR."

"Honey, do you remember how hard it was to teach me how to record *Hart Beat*? I don't think I could do that without you there to show me. I'm sorry, you'll have to just wait a few more weeks." That seems to be the final word.

"I'm hungry," Anne says, breaking the tension.

"Let's walk back towards your gran and see if she's ready for lunch," Dad says, definitively. That seems to draw a line under our conversation.

†

The weather starts to change as we munch on our sandwiches – crusts on – and reminds me of the remains we threw away on the train journey down to Devon. That day feels ages ago. I don't know how I should feel about Dad leaving. During the first few days we were here, I would have given anything for him to suddenly turn up and surprise us. But right now, I feel some slight relief that he's going home. I have unfinished business here, and I think I appreciate he has unfinished business at home. I hope we both sort things out quickly, as in before he brings Mum down to visit.

We're all a bit quiet on the ride back to Smuggler's Cove. Plenty for us to think about. Plenty of confusing and mixed feelings. Why can't things be simple again? I wish I could turn back the clock and stop myself kissing Beth.

Dad pulls up in the car park, and Grandma, Anne, and I disembark from the car.

"I think I'm going to try and get a head start on the traffic," Dad says, like he can't leave us quickly enough. "I packed my bag up earlier. If I've left anything in the caravan, I'll pick it up when we come back."

Anne starts to cry. "Is Mum really going to be herself again?" she asks.

"Yes, darling. The difference already is magnificent. I know she wants to focus on recovering, and she's looking forward to seeing you both and telling you she loves you in person," Dad replies.

"That's good to hear, love," Grandma chips in. "In the meantime, I'll take care of my girls. We'll telephone to that college and tell them they'd be fools not to let Robyn in this year."

To Autumn

"Thank you," Dad and I say at the same time. We all laugh.

"Love you, Dad, and Mum. Make sure you tell her I said that," I say. I want to add a plea for him to tell her I've had a boyfriend and I'm not going to be gay anymore, but the words don't come out.

Grandma puts her arms around our shoulders, although she can barely reach mine, and pulls us back half a step as Dad starts the car.

"Love you. All of you," Dad says, through the window.

"Drive safely, John." Grandma's words follow Dad as he waves the back of his hand to us and drives on.

Chapter Nineteen

I wake up on Saturday morning as though I'm coming out of a fog. The stress of the last few days is dislodging from my stomach and everywhere else I've clenched it in. The news that Mum will be coming to visit in two weeks' time lingers at the back of my mind. Anne's gentle snoring above me has me move about quietly as I manoeuvre out of bed.

I make myself a cup of tea, trying not to wake anyone else in the process. I want some time alone with my thoughts. Two weeks. That's how long I have to extinguish all of the fires I've caused. I'm scared that doing anything will only enflame the embers, as that seems to be my pattern. Why are good intentions not enough? I don't want to hurt anyone, but everything I do causes trouble.

Should I try and make amends with Dean? Will he even let me? I know that seeing me kissing Autumn will have hurt his feelings. I also know that he has the power to make things really difficult for both of us, and there's no good reason for him to not do that, except for the fact that I think he is a good person. I could apologise, try to explain, be honest about my exam results and even the reasons why I did badly. Maybe he'd understand better that I'm just a bit fucked up and none of it has anything to do with him. Apart from the fact that I used him, which was unfair of me. I allowed him to believe I was interested in him and led him on to think we might be in a relationship. That was selfish of me. But I only did that to help Mum get better, didn't I? Or was it more about soothing my guilt? Which didn't work and ended up creating even more. I'll find him and talk to him, and maybe he'll understand, especially if I tell him the truth about Mum. If he's willing to listen.

†

Grandma suggests the beach for the day, as we haven't been for a while. Because Saturday is turnover day – which means the holiday makers who've been here for a week go home and new arrivals come in their place – the beach is usually quieter. I know Autumn usually has a Saturday shift at the pool so she's unlikely to be there. And maybe the Jacksons'll be there and I could talk to Dean. If not, I'll volunteer for the washing up tonight. The sooner I try and talk to him, hopefully, the better I'll feel.

We set up camp in our usual spot, a little bit of shelter from the dunes behind. I'm glad we don't have one of those windbreakers to try and set up. All the other families that bring them seem to spend hours putting them up and then have to rejig them about every ten minutes or so.

Grandma plonks into her deckchair, and Anne and I set the towels out for us. We've worked out the trick of laying them out by leaning into the breeze, rather than working against it, although today, the breeze is almost non-existent.

Anne sets to work on her sandcastle. We've arrived early, for us, anyway, and there's hardly anyone else here. Time for a swim, then some Keats while I keep an eye on whether Dean and his family turn up. At least swimming will keep me busy. I do wonder whether Dean will have said anything to his parents already.

The water is not as cold as usual, thanks to a few days of sunnier weather. I lie back and float, letting the soft waves carry me to and fro. The current is mild. I relax and close my eyes. Seagulls bleat above me. The saltwater holds me steady, and I dangle the tips of my fingers into the soothing sea. The sun pulses down, warming my belly and thighs. I wish I could dissolve and drift all the way to Spain.

†

To Autumn

The waves become a bit too choppy to stay afloat without effort, so instead I flip over and stretch my arms and legs out into a swim. I ease my way back, level with Grandma and Anne, and spot that Anne isn't playing alone anymore. Jamie is with her. Which means the Jacksons are here. I strain my eyes to find their basecamp, which is just to the right of Grandma. Three bodies. Dean is there. It doesn't look like he's making his way towards the sea, which means I'm going to have to go to him if I want to make this talk happen. Perhaps I can ask him to come down to the water with me, and then we could chat in private. This isn't a conversation for the adults to hear.

    I ease out of the water and walk slowly back up to the group. Knowing I have to talk to Dean and actually wanting to are definitely not the same thing.

    "Hi, love," Grandma says, drawing everyone's attention to me. "Enjoy your dip?"

    "Hi everyone. Yes thanks. The water's almost warm. I wondered if you wanted to come in with me, Dean?" I hope that my face is sunned enough already to stop my blushes being obvious. Dean's parents nudge each other but keep their faces locked in the same smiles that greeted me. I can't tell whether this is a good or a bad thing.

    Dean looks at me, not replying. Grandma and the Jacksons are watching us. Seconds pass by, and I wonder what Dean is thinking. Whether he knows I'm about to confess all and gently break up with him, whether he thinks I've come crawling back for a second chance, whether he just wants to tell everyone here what he saw on Thursday night.

"Okay," he finally says. We walk down to the shore in silence.

†

"So." Great opener, Robyn. Dean replies with silence and an interest in the sea washing in over his toes.

"I guess I need to talk, to explain," I say, and he chokes out a grunt. "Fair enough, you don't want to make this easy for me. I deserve that. I just wanted you to know. What you saw, wasn't what it looked like." Dean turns to me at last, eyebrows raised. He takes a few more steps forward and I follow. "I mean it. I was having a bad day. I've had a bad year if I'm honest. That's kind of why we're here, Anne and me. My mum and dad weren't working abroad." Dean stops at the point where the water starts to become deep, then drops forward to start treading water. I copy him. He's really trying to make this hard for me.

"So, what really happened, was that Mum was in hospital. She nearly died. Dad was spending all of his time looking after her. Then it came to exams, and I knew I was going to do badly. I couldn't concentrate. I pretty much failed everything except for English. That's why Dad drove down on Thursday, to bring my results, and to tell us Mum might be getting better. So, I was emotional."

"Isn't it a good thing, your mum getting better?" Dean says, wearing an unforgiving sarcasm in his undertone.

"Yes! It is, but…" I have to find a way to explain that things are more complicated than just that. "Anyway, on Thursday night I was spilling it all out to Autumn because she found me in such a state. And I guess I was a bit confused because she was being nice to me and supporting me. And that's when you saw us." I know I am speaking too quickly, but I just want the words out of me and end the telling part of this conversation.

Dean lets his words out slowly. "Right. What I saw was her giving you support was it?"

"No. What you saw was…me doing something I shouldn't have because I was in a bad place."

"Why did you want to tell me all this?" Dean asks, still very calm with his words, still not looking at me.

"I wanted to explain, so…"

"So that I don't go round telling everyone you two were lezzing it up?" he asks, finally turning his face towards mine in a kind of challenge.

"No! Well, yes, partly. But, really, I wanted to apologise to you. I know it must have been a surprise." The words catch in my throat as it's clear that Dean doesn't want to hear any of this.

"What's a surprise is that you are a liar. I thought you were different." His honesty surprises me and pierces the moment.

"I'm sorry. You didn't deserve that." I don't have any more words.

"No. That's the first true thing you've said. I don't think I want to be friends anymore. I'll think about keeping your secret. Secrets, I mean."

With that, he catches a wave and body surfs back into the shore. I stay treading water, repeating the conversation with each crest of water passing through me. If I stay here long enough perhaps the tide will swallow me.

To Autumn

Chapter Twenty

Grandma and Anne do their best to cheer me up. They don't ask why I'm down, and maybe the GCSE failure is enough of a reason, without the need to understand all of the other problems in my life.

"First thing Monday morning, we'll phone that college, Robyn, and see what we can do." Grandma's taken it upon herself to lead the charge in reinstating my future. I am happy to hand the reins to her.

"Sounds good," I say. I'm focusing on enjoying spending time with the two of them, since they're the only people in my life I haven't alienated myself from.

"Why don't we head to Totnes for some shopping today?" Grandma asks. I think she has run out of ideas about how to lift my mood.

"Yes, please!" Anne says. I'm still not used to words coming from her.

"Good. Go and wash then, girls, and we'll head out when you're ready." A day off site is probably a good idea. Definitely reduces the chances of bumping into anyone I don't want to see. I've managed to avoid Autumn since the kiss, and Dean has avoided me since yesterday, and I am glad. If I just keep to myself and Grandma and Anne, there won't be the chance for any more drama.

†

Grandma's tin Fiesta bounces over the holiday park's long potholed driveway. Just outside the entrance, there's a bus stop. Autumn and her girlfriend, and a suitcase, are standing there. Grandma stops next to them and rolls down her window.

"Hello, dears," she says. The concrete block in my stomach returns. What is Grandma doing? I slink down in the back but keep an angle where I can watch this interaction.

"Hi, Mrs Gale," Autumn says, but not with her usual casual joy. Her girlfriend's face looks tear stained. She must be sad to be leaving.

"Where are you two off to, then?" Grandma's curiosity is not subtle.

To Autumn

"I'm taking my," Autumn looks awkward, she seems to have misplaced her Aussie cool. "Uh, my friend Haley to the station."

"Get in! I'll give you both a lift, save you dragging that suitcase on the bus. Squeeze over, Robyn," Grandma says, as though she's just made the best suggestion ever.

"No, that's okay, Mrs Gale. The bus is due any minute."

"Nonsense," Grandma says. She's already out of the car and opening the boot. She picks up the case and places it in there. Then she folds forward her seat and gestures for Autumn and Hayley to get in the car. "Our pleasure, isn't it, girls?"

I turn and face the passenger side window, squeezing up as closely as I can to the door. Autumn gets in first, taking the middle. Hayley slowly steps in and takes the other window seat.

"Thank you, Mrs Gale," Autumn says.

"My pleasure, dear. And what's your friend's name?"

"Hayley," they both say at the same time.

"Lovely. My quiet granddaughters here are Anne and Robyn. Let's be off." And with that, Grandma swerves out into the road, narrowly missing the bus as it approaches the stop.

†

After fifteen minutes of excruciating questioning by Grandma, we all know Hayley's life story. Except for why she has tear smudges on her face. We pull up to the drop off zone at the station. They clamber clumsily out of the car, while Grandma opens the boot.

"Thank you, Mrs Gale, that was very kind," Hayley says when she's taken her case out of the boot.

"No problem at all, and make sure Autumn sees you off safely. I'm sure we'll see you at the pool, Autumn." They both wave and then turn towards the station, hips bumping as they walk up the ramp to the entrance.

"Our good deed for the day." Grandma's final words as we drive off.

I can see their reflection in the rear-view mirror. Autumn's hand on Hayley's back. This really looks like she ended things. Not. I'm not the only liar it seems.

†

We weave in and out of second-hand bookshops and hippy-dippy stalls selling crystals and dream catchers. That's all Totnes seems to offer, but the town and shops are packed. I'd forgotten what it was like to feel that crush and cram while walking along a pavement. I haven't really missed London, despite being homesick for Mum and Dad and my friends. For the first moment since we left home, I feel a pang for a life where I find it easy to stay anonymous, be one among many, and out of the limelight.

Grandma declares she wants to treat us all to a cream tea. This is a local speciality I've been hearing about all holiday, as I've been catching snippets of families'

To Autumn

conversations. It seems to be the thing to do in Devon. I'm not sure I'll like cream in my tea, but it means we can sit down for a bit.

"My favourite!" says Anne, and it dawns on me that Grandma has been doing nice things with her all holiday while I've been moping with my books in the caravan or at the pool.

The tea house is quaint, with heavy wooden beams and lead-lined windows. We are seated at a square table all set out with posh napkins and cutlery. I wonder why we need cutlery for tea. Grandma orders and we wait. The place is packed, and all around us teaspoons are clanging against porcelain cups.

My view is directly facing a window which looks out onto the street, capturing clusters of people walk by and creating a strange contrast to the tea-house decor in their modern-day clothes. Inside, it feels like we're sitting in a period drama and ought to be wearing lace and bonnets. A familiar figure crosses the window from left to right. Autumn. Alone. She looks different, shoulders hunched, head down. She doesn't look in, and Grandma doesn't see her, but once she passes, her image stays.

A waitress, dressed in the period attire I'd been imagining we all should be wearing, brings over a cake tier full of scones and little bowls of cream and jam, then returns with a huge tea pot and jug of milk. Grandma and Anne each take a scone, halve it, then layer it with jam and then the thick cream on top using tiny spoons. Suddenly it makes a lot of sense why this is something everyone talks about down here. I pick up my own scone, which is still warm, and full of sultanas. I look around, some people at other tables have put the cream on first before the jam, which I think looks better. As I draw some cream from the little bowl, Grandma and Anne look at me with horror.

"What?" I ask.

"Jam first!" Anne says. I can't understand why it matters.

"Robyn, if you want to do it the other way, you go ahead," Grandma says, giving Anne a silencing look. The only thing I can think to do is try both styles on each half of the scone. I prefer the cream first, but I think it's best not to share that.

†

I'm glad I made the effort to come with Grandma and Anne. Once our stomachs are full and there's only tea leaves left in the pot, Grandma pays, and we leave. There's been a long gap since Autumn walked past the window, and I hope that means we won't bump into her again.

CHAPTER TWENTY-ONE

The following day we are back to business. Anne and I clear away the breakfast plates while Grandma busies herself in her room. She's clanging about but I have no idea what she's up to. She finally enters the galley looking triumphant.

"I've found some extra change for the phone, and we'll take a notebook and pen," she declares. She sounds like we should know what she's talking about. When neither Anne nor I reply, she continues, "so we can call up the college and sort out your enrolment, Robyn."

Oh. That job. I didn't think she had been serious when she said she was going to call them.

"I don't have a number, though," I argue, willing to say anything to get out of doing this. This can wait until I'm home. Probably.

"No fear, we'll call directory enquiries first. Hence I brought extra coins and some paper." She really doesn't want to give me any inch of this not happening.

"Okay. But, we have to call from the phone box. Do you think it's fair if we hog it for hours?"

"I'm sure people will understand if we explain." Great. "And that's why we're going now – first thing. There won't be a queue."

The three of us walk towards the phone, weaving in and out of mobile homes. Grandma was right, of course, there isn't a queue at 9.30am on a Monday morning.

"Right, Anne, you hold the coin purse open and be ready to pass over coins for me to top up the call. Robyn, you take the notebook and pen and write down everything I say. First of all, we'll dial 192." Am I supposed to write that down? She puts in a twenty pence piece and dials.

"Hello. Please could I have the number for South West London College? Robyn, quick, be ready to write this down. Yes, I'm ready. The main switchboard, please. Robyn. Right, 0181, yes, 555, yes, 4567. Shall I read that back to you? No. Okay, thank you." She puts the phone down and takes a coin from Anne. "Robyn, can you read the number out for me as I dial, please?" I feel like I am in a sitcom

To Autumn

episode, "The One Where the Teenager Wishes She Could Be Sucked Into a Hole In The Ground".

I read out the number slowly to match Grandma's dialling speed. I wonder who she is going to speak to if this is the main switchboard. She can't exactly ask the receptionist to approve my admission into college.

"Ringing," Grandma says. We wait. We wait a bit longer. "I might have to hang up and try – oh, hello there, I wonder if you can help me?" Grandma has pulled out a telephone voice from nowhere.

"Thank you, dear. I am hoping to speak to someone who can help me sort out my granddaughter's place there starting in September. She didn't do very well in her exams, but it wasn't her fault." Cringe. Pause. "Right, I need to speak to Deputy Principal Khan." Grandma signals at me to write the name down. "Are you able to put me through?" Pause. "Her secretary, right, yes please." Pause. "I'm on hold." Pause. "Hello? Yes, my name is Gloria Gale, and I'm the grandmother of a student hoping to start at the college in September. She's called Robyn Gale. Yes. Due to a family emergency, she wasn't able to do her best in her GCSEs." Pause. "All of them. It was a big emergency. Except for English. Anyway, I'm hoping to find a way for Mrs Khan to let her start with her friends, rather than repeat the year at school." Pause.

A couple of kids start a queue behind us. Grandma takes out two coins from the purse Anne is holding and slots them into the phone. The kids leave the queue. "Okay, yes,

I'm still here. Right. Okay, in exceptional circumstances, it may be possible. What are exceptional circumstances?" Pause. "Yes, I think she would qualify. What do we have to do?" She waves her hand at me again. "Robyn, make a note. Write a letter to Mrs Khan, outlining the results, the situation, and how it impacted her. Ask the school to write a reference giving her mock results and predicted grades. Yes. And what options might there be for her?" Pause. "Right, thank you very much. And your name is Judy Smith, Mrs Khan's secretary. Thank you. And could I have the college postal address, please?" Grandma takes the pen and paper from me and writes down the address. "Okay, goodbye then."

She hangs up the phone and smiles. What is she smiling for? It sounds like we have a lot of work to do before I'll know whether I can start college.

"Let's go back home and I'll explain it all to you. I need a cup of tea. But I have good news." Grandma strides off before either Anne or I have a chance to say anything, and we quick step to catch up with her.

†

We enter the caravan, and Grandma signals to the kettle. "Put that on, will you, dear?" She sits down and reads through the notes I made.

"We'll have to call your school as well, Robyn. I'd like to that this afternoon."

Might just be easier to repeat the year. This is becoming complicated.

"Is there a specific teacher it would be best to talk to?"

I doubt anyone will be there during the holidays, unless they are about during the results period.

"Just ask for the headteacher's secretary," I say. That's Michelle's mum. I'm sure she is there during the exam results weeks. But that means Michelle and Tanith will find out about my results disaster. At least being here, I don't have to go through the pain of having to hide my failure while I find out how well everyone else did.

"I fancy a walk if that's okay," I say when I've downed the last of the tea. It scalds my tongue. "Along the beach. I'll be fine on my own."

"I'll come!" Anne says. We've hardly spent any time alone together since the first week here. She's been having fun with Grandma all the time, while I've been busy fucking up my life.

"Off you go then," Grandma says, barely paying us any attention. "I'll see if I can get through to the school and then start on the statements. Back for lunch please."

I'm surprised but happy she's allowed us to head out on our own. I haven't walked enough this holiday. That's definitely a Mum-driven activity.

We walk past the playground and the bench of my nightmares. I wish Dean had never showed it to me. Up on the dunes, the sun is peeking out from behind white fluffy clouds. The beach is busy. I always forget how hard it is to walk in sand, and suggest we head down to the shoreline, where the wet sand is firmer. I take off my sandals and let the cold tide wash over my feet. Anne copies me.

"What happened? With you and Dean, and you and Autumn?" she asks.

I'm still not used to her speaking, and I'm definitely not used to her asking me questions this boldly. Our lives are so separate at home.

"I don't know what you mean," I say, with no desire to spill my guts to my little sister.

"You were friends with both of them, and now you don't talk to them." She's observant.

"What are you talking about? I spoke to Dean on Saturday, and Autumn was in our car yesterday." I'm both horrified and impressed she's made this observation and called me out on it. I'm determined to throw her off the scent of what's really going on.

"You and Dean went to swim together, and then when you came back you both looked in a bad mood and didn't speak to each other for the rest of the day. I haven't seen you talking to Autumn for weeks, even when she was in the car yesterday." Silent but deadly is Anne.

"Just because you haven't seen it doesn't mean I haven't spoken to them." My last word. "That's not important, anyway. Not as important as realising that I've hardly spent any time at all with you and Grandma this summer. I didn't even figure out you were talking again. But

Grandma did. I feel like I'm missing out with you two. So, it doesn't matter about them, because I'm going to spend more time with you instead. Because I want to, not because I'm not friends with Dean or Autumn anymore."

"That would be nice," Anne says, "I've missed you. And Grandma's different to what you first think, once you know her."

"How are you so wise?" I ask, taken aback by her insights.

"When you don't talk much, you hear a lot."

The breeze is making the waves come in a bit harder, and the spray is as high as our shorts.

"We'd better turn back soon," I say, or Grandma will be on the warpath for us missing lunch.

"She's not that bad," Anne says. "I'm glad she's helping you sort out college."

"Me too." We turn around, the midday sun causing us to squint. The bottom of our shorts are soaking, but the water on our legs feels pleasant. We have to dodge lots of children being teased by the tide, not yet brave enough to take the plunge in. The roar of the sea softens the sounds of their shrieks when a wave crashes harder than expected. I wish being splashed by waves was the only thing I needed to worry about.

†

When we arrive back at the caravan, Grandma is sitting at the table writing furiously. She doesn't look up as we walk in, she's deep in concentration. There's no lunch in sight. I open the fridge and take out some ham, cheese, and tomatoes for sandwiches. Anne and I make three chunky doorstops and a jug of orange squash. By the time we take things over to the table, Grandma is still writing, but the furious pen action is slowing down.

"Don't spill anything on these papers," Grandma orders, pulling the pile of filled pages towards her. "Just let me finish this sentence and I'll update you."

We munch on our sandwiches while she scribbles for a few minutes longer until she finally puts the pen down and exhales a long breath. She takes the sheets of paper and assembles them into an orderly pile.

"You made lunch! Thank you, girls," Grandma says. She must have really been focusing on whatever she was writing to not have noticed us faffing about in the kitchen.

"No problemo," I respond. "I take it that means the call with the school went well? What do we need to do? Do you think the college is going to let me in?" I hadn't realised how important this is to me. I'd been completely focused on everyone finding out about the results.

Through a mouthful of bread and cheese, Grandma reports that there are several options to being allowed into college. One is that I repeat year 11 there. Another, which sounds more promising, is that I start my English Lit A level, revise for the November retakes, and if I pass those, join my other A Level classes in January. If I catch up, I could do my exams with everyone else. If I don't, I can take all of my

To Autumn

exams at the end of the two years rather than at the end of each module.

As long as the school officially backs up that I would have most likely done better in the exams if I wasn't going through deep stuff at home and agrees that I'll be able to work hard enough to catch up, I'm all set. Grandma says she spoke to Michelle's mum, and that she thinks the Head will agree and be happy to write in support of whatever option I choose. I can't believe everyone is being nice to me and not making me feel like I'm a total failure. Grandma has been writing a letter of support on my behalf, too. I'll need to write one for myself, to say that I really do want to go to college and that I think I am ready to do the retakes and work hard on catching up. After all these months of secrecy and fear of the results ruining my life, it seems that things might turn out alright after all. Thanks to Grandma.

Chapter Twenty-two

The sun returns after those earlier stormy weeks. Grandma, Anne, and I hang out together a lot, either going down to the beach for a few hours, visiting some cool places in south Devon like Dartington, or teaching Anne new card games. No Pass the Pigs or Uno, thank goodness. Grandma bought a National Trust membership for us to walk around pretty gardens and park for free at big houses. Sometimes, her friend Mr Hooper comes with us.

A weight has lifted now that college is likely to be a go. Grandma and I posted our letters last Tuesday, and the school said they would do the same. We need to give them time to look at everything. Grandma said we could try and call this Friday, which is the start of our final weekend here, because she thinks all the staff'll return after the bank holiday weekend.

    The holiday park is busier than normal this week because of the bank holiday weekend. I can't believe we've reached the last week of the holidays already. Dad is bringing Mum down to stay with us on Friday, too. We've spoken to her on the phone a few more times. She sounds like Mum again. She's been home since last Saturday. I wonder what it feels like for her, being home again. I'm scared that if she's not fully, truly better, it will only take a small event to send her back into the hospital. Or worse. Do we all have to be extra careful? I mean, not just me staying away from kissing girls, but also not raising our voices at each other, and being more helpful around the house? Will things ever be normal again?

    I don't appreciate the irony that now I've finally started to enjoy being in Devon, it's nearly time for us to leave. I'm also sad that we've wasted too many years not coming here to visit and not knowing Grandma as well as we are now starting to. I don't long for everything to simply return to how it was before, there are changes we should make as a family. Having college to look forward to is positive though, a fresh start at home, even if I have to focus on the exam resits to start with.

    "We'll need to start organising ourselves for the weekend," Grandma says, snapping me out of my wandering thoughts. "Your parents can sleep on the fold out double in here, but that means we should tidy up a bit to make sure there's enough room for them. It'll be like the old days."

Anne and I pick up the stray books and games we've grown used to having scattered around the lounge. I like how comfortable we've become here, just the three of us. The space will feel full when Mum and Dad arrive. The thought makes me want to escape.

For the first time in a long time, I ask, "Can we go to the pool this afternoon?"

Grandma and Anne both look shocked. We've avoided it with an unspoken agreement since Dad was here.

"If that's what you want," Grandma says. Anne nods. I just need to swim for lengths and lengths.

†

After lunch we head over to the pool with a bag full of towels, goggles, books, lotion and Grandma's deck chair. The weather and a busy week mean we have to scramble to find a space big enough for the three of us. No chance of shade. I don't care, I put goggles on and dive straight in. I don't even look to see who is on lifeguard duty.

I've missed this. I've missed that sensation of total submersion and feeling like I am in another world; that something else is carrying the weight of my life for me. I stretch out and glide long front crawl strokes. Length after length, turn after turn, my mind finally switches off and focuses on the next stroke and avoiding the slower swimmers in the lane. When my calves start to ache, I know I need to stop. I move into the main pool section and allow myself to float but the pool is too busy to stay like that for very long. I turn upright and scan the scene. I catch Anne at the shallow end, splashing. She's not alone. My toes curl when I see she's trying to soak Jamie. I look over to Grandma, and she's now sitting with the Jacksons. Three of them. Before I can turn my head and body around to look towards the lifeguard station, a whistle shrills. Autumn. Why did I think coming here would be a good idea?

I edge towards the steps, knowing I'll have to climb out sooner or later, and given my legs are in a pre-cramp state, sooner it will be. I find a spot in the shallow end to sit on the ledge for a minute, watching Anne and Jamie. They head over to me and both start splashing chaotically. I return a big swipe of water and they move off.

Someone sits next to me.

"I suppose you come here just to enjoy the view," Dean says. The concrete block in my stomach anchors me to the spot.

"I come here to swim," I respond, trying to sound calm.

"I saw you. Showing off for your Baywatch babe."

"I wasn't… I don't have to explain to you. I was just swimming," I say, trying not to sound as defensive as I feel.

"Your grandma said your parents are coming to visit tomorrow. She didn't mention they'd been out of the country. In fact, she said that they've been in London all summer," Dean says. "You really are a big lezzie liar, aren't you?"

"It's complicated," I say. He doesn't deserve the truth while he's in this mood.

"I'm sure it is. Doesn't matter who you hurt." He swims off and I feel a little bad even though he's behaving like an arse. I wasn't fair to him, and I haven't been able to apologise properly because that would mean telling him everything. I can't do that.

I look over to the lifeguard's chair. Autumn is looking my way and gives a small wave and a smile. I can't return it. I climb out of the pool and grab my towel, drying off quickly as the shade has a chill to it.

†

We stop and shower on our way back to the caravan. The warm water is a chance to wash off the conversation with Dean. At the caravan we change into cosy clothes while Grandma cooks dinner. There's a pile of photos on the coffee table. I take a look. They are the photos I found on our first day here. Anne and I pore over them. Grandma and Aunty Di's smiling faces peer out, then a very young-looking Mum and Dad hold a baby right here in the lounge.

"Is this me?" I ask. I haven't seen this photo before.

"Who else would it be?" Grandma says.

"Me?" Anne says.

To Autumn

"No, your parents never brought Anne here. After. Well, you know. You didn't come back here after your sixth birthday, Robyn."

I don't remember. I don't have any vivid memories of being here before, just a sense of familiarity of certain places in the holiday park.

"Why?" No one has ever explained why we haven't seen Grandma very often since Anne was born.

"Your mum and dad haven't talked to you about this?" Grandma says, genuinely surprised.

"About what? Did something happen?" Are there answers to questions I didn't even know I could ask?

"When your Mum was in hospital, after Anne was born, you stayed here with me. Just us two. We had a wonderful time. It wasn't long after Di had passed away and you were missing your parents, but we were great friends." Why don't I remember? Why was Mum in hospital?

"Mum was in hospital? Did something happen during the birth? Was Anne okay?" The questions flood out, now I know which ones to ask.

"It's not my place to say, if your parents haven't talked to you both about it," Grandma says mysteriously.

I'm confused, like I've discovered a missing piece of the puzzle of my life, a piece I hadn't even realised was lost under the sofa for all these years.

"Given everything we've been through this year, I think we can handle it, right, Anne?" I say.

"Yes," Anne says, and puts down the photos she's been looking at.

"Okay, set the table for dinner, and I'll tell you while we eat. I'm almost finished here." Grandma is retrieving chicken from the oven and has mixed a damp lettuce salad. Anne and I speedily take out the plates and cutlery and mix a jug of orange squash.

Grandma brings the plates over, then sits down. Anne squeezes ketchup all over her food.

"Well?" I ask, trying my hardest not to sound impatient and rude.

"After your mum had Anne, she had post-natal depression – which can happen when a baby's born and sets the hormonal balance wonky for mothers. Your mum's case was serious, she had to stay in hospital about a month. Anne stayed with her, as she was breastfeeding, and because the hospital thought it would be important for her recovery and to bond with Anne. Of course, your dad wanted to visit them every day, and to help out he asked me to look after you, Robyn. And I didn't realise that I needed you as much as you needed me. I was still grieving for Di.

"Then, your mum started to improve and was put on medication to help her. After about five weeks, your parents came and collected you. I didn't want you to go, I wanted you to stay and live with me. I think that shocked your parents and seemed to put a wall between us all."

"They haven't told us any of this," I say. "Right, Anne?"

"Nope." She's focused on smothering her chicken in ketchup.

Then a realisation hits me. "Wait, Mum has been ill like she is now, before?" I ask.

"I know about that time, and this time. I couldn't say about any other episodes. You'll have to talk to your parents about it if you want to know more." I'm boiling with anger. Anger because they kept this from me, anger because they're the reason we haven't seen Grandma enough, anger because Anne and I've been treated like little kids this whole time.

"But that means..." I trail off. That means it might not be my fault. Maybe Mum didn't drive into the wall because she saw me kissing Beth.

Chapter Twenty-three

We finish our dinners, and the conversation is left sitting at the table. I take the dishes down to the shower block to wash them up. Questions and anger are festering in me, and I bang around the plates in the sink, scrubbing them extra hard today.

"Careful, you'll break something," Dean's smug voice trails behind him. "Had some bad news?" he asks. I've no idea what he's talking about.

"Mind your own," I shout, wiping the dishes quickly, stacking them back in the box not-quite-dry. He doesn't retort.

To Autumn

Grandma doesn't comment on the still-damp plates, but I give them another towel off before I put them back in the cupboard.

"Shall we go down to the club house tonight, for the end of season raffle? Anne's happy to come along."

"Sure," I say. Anything other than thinking and talking.

†

We stroll down towards the complex.

"Can we call Mum and Dad?" Anne asks, as we approach the phone box.

"I suppose we can have a quick call just to check what time they're planning to arrive tomorrow," Grandma says, and draws out a ten pence piece.

I'll be happy never to see silver coins again. Next time we visit, Dad can buy us a mobile phone to call home with.

I stand slightly to the side, not wanting to be passed the phone. They keep it quick and confirm that they're going to set off early and try and reach us by lunch time. Great.

I've wanted this moment to come for so long, but now it feels tainted with the secrets Mum and Dad have been keeping from us.

We walk on to the club house and as we are approaching, Mr Hooper comes power walking out of the doors. He makes a beeline for us.

"I was just coming to see you," he pants.

"We've popped down for the raffle," Grandma says.
"I need to talk to you. You and Robyn, Gloria." He sounds serious, I wonder what's happened. "Can we go somewhere private? Your home." He's not asking, and he's strangely agitated.

He hurries us back to the caravan and we all sit down.

"This might be a bit delicate, perhaps little Anne could give us some space."

This is serious. Is it something to do with Mum's visit? Grandma asks Anne to go and read in our room, as if the flimsy panelling will block out the sound of our words.

"I want to talk to you about Autumn. She's been asked to leave her job here because someone reported her kissing a guest. You see, there are strict rules against staff having relationships with holiday makers."

I wonder if they mean Hayley, when she came to visit. Did someone see them kissing and assume Hayley was a guest? Or has there been another girl under Autumn's spell?

"She's been fired?" Grandma asks, pointing out the obvious.

"Not exactly, but the management did ask her to resign. She admitted it was true, you see. Robyn, she said that she kissed you, when you were having a conversation about your GCSE results. She said that you weren't complicit, that she kissed you and you pulled away, that she misread your closeness, that she's sorry. Is that what happened?"

To Autumn

"Who reported this?" I ask, the words scratching my throat. "It wasn't me! I don't want her to be in trouble."

"It was another guest. He said he saw what happened. Autumn confirmed it. We just wanted to hear from you and check whether you're okay?" he says, concern coating his voice.

I nod. What should I do? Autumn's losing her job because of me.

"Robyn didn't tell me anything about this," Grandma says softly. "I knew you'd had some sort of falling out, but didn't imagine it was this."

I'm waiting for the tabloid-inspired homophobia-tinged sentiments about how disgusting Autumn is and how wrong she must be for doing that to me.

"Is that what happened, Robyn?" Mr Hooper asks me.

I can't speak. I just nod, in silence.

"Okay, well I had to check, in case there was something else to it. The person who reported it seemed very keen to cause trouble for Autumn. She's devastated of course. I've spoken to her. She's been allowed the weekend to pack up, and she'll be on her way on Monday."

Why has she taken the fall for this? How could Dean have done that to her? She hasn't done anything to him. Except be the obstacle in his way to me. Is that what this is all about? If only I could tell the truth. I really wish I could. But I can't risk it, not with Mum and Dad visiting tomorrow.

"Are you okay, Robyn? Did she hurt you?" Grandma asks.

"No! It was nothing. That's why I didn't say anything to you. It was nothing, just a misunderstanding. Really. She doesn't deserve to lose her job over it." That's the best version of events I can bear to muster.

"The rules are there for a reason, and all the staff are told about them when they start. They're strictly enforced to avoid situations like this," Mr Hooper says, although he doesn't have much conviction in his voice. "I have to go back to run the raffle. I just thought it might be easier if you heard this from me, rather than the site manager."

"Thank you," Grandma says, and stands up to see him out. She kisses his cheek, and then he leaves. She sighs.

"Robyn, I think there was a reason your dad sent you and Anne to me this summer, beyond trying to help out while he's looking after your Mum." Grandma opens our bedroom door to let Anne out. She's vibrating with light snores, asleep on the bed.

Grandma picks up the photos from the coffee table, and skims through them. She pulls out one of her and Di holding me outside the mobile home.

"I miss her. She'd know what to say right now. She was always good with your dad, she loved your mum, too. She was overjoyed when you came along. I wanted your parents to name you after her, she was already starting to go downhill when you were born."

I have very vague memories of Aunty Di. I wish I could remember more.

To Autumn

"That's why Anne is called Anne – in honour of Diane. Shame Di didn't have the chance to meet her, too. She would've loved having two granddaughters." Grandma takes a tissue and dabs at her eyes.

"You mean great nieces?" I ask, thinking Grandma has made a slip of the tongue. "Aunty Di was your sister?"

"This is what happens when people aren't honest from the outset," Grandma mutters to herself, snuffling into the soggy tissue. "Actually, she wasn't my sister. Aunty Di was my... well I'm not sure there's a word for it. Life partner might be the best way to describe it."

My jaw hits the carpet underneath us. Grandma is a lesbian?

"We were both widowed quite young. She lost her husband in the war. They hadn't had children. It wasn't common for women to remarry in those days. And then, when your Grandfather Jonathan had his heart attack, there was just me and John. I met Di here. We both booked a holiday for the same week in August 1962. We were seated together for dinner one night at the old restaurant; two women on their own, I suppose they thought we wouldn't mind. And we didn't. We were instant friends. Over time, it developed into something more. Neither of us were bothered about remarrying. We enjoyed each other's company, your father adored her, and life was much easier for both of us as a pair instead of alone." Grandma stops, catching her breath after this monologue.

"I didn't know," is all I can think to say. Grandma, my Grandma, had a female life partner.

"Well, it wasn't like it is today, back then. You didn't talk about it. We just lived our lives. Most people assumed we were sisters. We didn't contradict them. Anyway, when we moved in together and no longer needed two houses, we sold Di's house and decided to buy the mobile home here, where we first met."

I'm finding more and more loose puzzle pieces under the sofa of my life. Is this why I'm gay?

"Why did Dad send us here for the holidays? And not to Nonna and Pops' house?" They live much closer to Wimbledon and staying with them would have made a lot more sense.

"There's probably more than one reason why, but I think your dad was hoping you could talk to me. About what happened at home, with your friend." Dad knows about Beth? But he's never said anything to me. Which means the real reason he sent us here is because he blames me for what happened to Mum and wanted us to be as far away as possible.

"You know about that? Does Dad hate me? Is that why we're here?" I ask, trying to place all the pieces together.

"Robyn, your father doesn't hate you. But, yes, I think that has something to do with it, of course it does," Grandma says, still very gentle in her tone. "I realised something was going on between you and Autumn, but I thought it was just a little crush on your part."

Was I that obvious to everyone? No wonder Autumn picked up my vibe. I've been wandering around with my feelings for her tattooed on my forehead apparently. Mega cringe.

"I've messed everything up," I say, wanting to bury myself deep underground and not emerge until everyone has forgotten everything.

"You haven't done anything wrong, love," Grandma responds, and puts her arm around me. "Sixteen is a complicated time, but I promise you it does start to become easier, eventually."

I need to show Mum and Dad that they don't have to worry about me, that I can live my life without being gay. Having feelings for someone is all too messy anyway, I'll be better off on my own. That way I can't hurt anyone ever again.

"I'm tired," I say. I am exhausted with the information overload, and with the guilt I have over my actions.

"Let's have an early night then, we want to be refreshed for your parents' arrival tomorrow."

Shit. I'd forgotten they were coming with the chaos of the last couple of hours. I hope I manage to calm down enough to sleep tonight.

Chapter Twenty-four

TGIF is a myth. I tossed and turned all night and wish I could sink under the blankets in my bunk for the rest of the day. Grandma wants us to call the college this morning and then we will be waiting for the arrival of Mum and Dad. Five weeks ago, I would have given anything to know that Mum is recovering and coming back to us, and that they would be coming for a visit. That feels like a lifetime ago.

Anne and Grandma are already up and about. I can hear their chatter and the kitchen cupboards opening and shutting. I don't think I could move, let alone eat, with the weight of the concrete block expanded to full capacity in my stomach today. Now I know the truth: that Dad sent us away because everything is my fault, and that Mum and Dad have

To Autumn

been keeping their own secrets from us all these years. I'm not in the mood for a happy family reunion. When did life become uber complicated?

The kettle clicks off to signal the end of boiling. I know it won't be long before Grandma calls me in for breakfast. A cup of tea might do something to help me anyway. I pull the blind up, and the day is overcast, a contrast from the last few days. Grabbing my hoodie, I step out of the bedroom, my curly hair defying gravity as it sticks up in every direction.

"Morning!" Grandma is especially cheery today.

"Hmmm." I yawn back to her.

"Morning, sleepy head," Anne joins in. I swallow a hot mouthful of tea, making my eyes water.

"We'll go to the phone box when you've had breakfast," Grandma announces, not giving me a choice to procrastinate.

I suppose I should just get it over with, know the outcome one way or the other. The fate of my future lies in the college's hands and until we find out their decision, there's nothing I can do.

"Sure," I say, forcing a smile.

†

At just after nine on a Friday morning, there's unsurprisingly no queue at the phone. There's nothing left standing between me and the news. Grandma take several twenty-pence pieces from Anne, who's holding the purse once again. I've been tasked with holding up a piece of paper with the phone number on it. Grandma managed to secure a direct number for Mrs Khan the Deputy Principal. This means we won't have to recount the situation to yet another stranger.

"Ringing," Grandma says, and her confidence and brazenness strikes me. She hasn't once shown any doubt that she could resolve this situation, no matter what it takes. "Mrs Khan, yes, Gloria Gale here." I'm both frustrated and relieved that I can only hear one side of the conversation. "We wondered whether you'd been able to come to a decision about Robyn starting with you this September." Pause.

"Okay, I see. Thank you." Pause. "And that's it? Do you need anything else from us?" Pause. "Thank you, Mrs Khan, I value your time and consideration of Robyn's circumstances."

I can't tell whether this is going well or badly.

Grandma puts the phone down, lets out a huge breath, then turns to Anne and me. The corners of her mouth flicker upwards, slowly growing into a huge beaming smile.

"Looks like you'll be Robyn Gale, college student, in just under two weeks' time," she says and gives me a big hug. "You're allowed to start your English A-Level and work on the resits for November." Anne joins in too and the three of us stand there, squeezing each other and bouncing up and down. Before I can stop them, tears fall.

"I'm very proud of you, Robyn," Grandma says.

I don't know why. "For what? Messing up and causing a massive stress for us all."

"For not giving up, for letting me help you, for doing what you needed to do without an attitude. You've righted your situation. That's very grown up." Grandma hands me a tissue from her sleeve.

I want to tell her the truth about Autumn. That I kissed her, not the other way around, and that Autumn should not lose her job over my lack of self-control.

"Thank you," is what I say instead.

"Wonderful, we have some good news to tell your parents," Grandma says.

"They'll be here soon!" Anne reminds us. Out of one frying pan, straight into another.

"They will. Robyn, do you want to go for a swim before lunch?" I do not.

"No thanks, Grandma, I think I'd just like to read my book of Keats' letters and hang out at home. If that's okay with you and Anne?" I don't want to be reminded of my guilt by being in a place where Autumn is supposed to be. Also, I need some time to think about what I'm going to say to Mum and Dad.

"Of course, dear. Anne, if you want to go the pool, I'm sure we can manage just the two of us." Anne agrees. We head back to the caravan, and they pick up their pool stuff. I pick up my Keats, the truly cool birthday present Grandma and Anne chose for me, and my Walkman so that I can play my other truly cool birthday present, the mix tape

Autumn gave me. Hopefully one or the other will help me figure out what to do.

They leave and I stretch out on the sofa. Finding time alone since we came to Devon has been a rarity, and I don't want to waste a second of this joy. Despite how much I want to relax and let my mind work on all of my problems magically like a computer processor, my brain still won't switch off.

Daydreams play out how conversations with Mum and Dad will go… in one version I confront them before they even have a chance to say "Hello". I cut them off, launching straight into "Why couldn't you be honest with us? Why didn't you tell us Mum has been in hospital with depression before, why not say the reason you wanted to be rid of us is because you blame me for what happened with Mum?"

And yet, I know I can't go in all guns blazing. I don't want to be blamed for setting Mum off on another downward spiral. I have to play it cool. In English class we read a poem by Philip Larkin, "This Be the Verse". I didn't understand the full meaning until now. Although everyone else was a bit silly about the swearing, I think they all kind of understood what it meant. I suppose in some ways, everyone's families are complicated. I mean, I'm glad my Mum isn't the school headteacher's secretary which is what Michelle has to put up with, but I often wish we could just be a family that doesn't have to deal with any big problems.

Then there's Autumn who unjustly lost her job. I can't believe Dean would have done that to her, she hasn't

To Autumn

done anything to him. I'm the person who hurt Dean, and I'm the person who kissed Autumn. Why didn't she tell the park manager it was me who was out of line, instead of taking the fall? If only there was a way to make it right without pushing Mum back over the edge. If Autumn leaves this weekend, there's a chance I won't be able to say goodbye, and that I'll never see her again.

If I can't talk to her, maybe I can write a letter to her. I don't have to send it, but it might be good to let out all of these feelings that have been building up, and to apologise. I tear out a page from Grandma's notebook and start writing, words flowing as I've barely put pen to paper.

Smugglers' Cove Holiday Park, Devon
Friday 29 August 1997
Dear Autumn,

I should have written this weeks ago. I wish had the courage to tell you how I really felt, and to have been honest with you from the start. I wanted to protect Mum and make sure she started to recover. I thought I had to lie. I thought that if I found a boyfriend, Mum would stop thinking I'm a lesbian and feel better again. She'd know I'm normal.

When we arrived here, and I first saw you at the pool, my whole body jumped. An electric charge went through me, and I knew I was in trouble. I tried to stay away from you. But it seemed like the harder I tried, the more our paths crossed, and deep down, I liked that. The more we got to know each other, the bigger my crush became.

I thought I had to push things with Dean to make it look like he was my boyfriend. That wasn't fair on him, or anyone else. Even though I thought I was doing it for the right reasons.

That night on the bench, when I found out my GCSE results and told you what had been going on in my life, I had never felt as safe as that. Talking to you, really being able to open up, felt incredible. There's no one else in my life I've felt I could be that honest with.

I don't know for sure who reported you. I have a feeling who it may have been, someone trying to get revenge. I'm sorry beyond measure that my mistake is costing you your job and your reputation. I shouldn't have kissed you. I don't know how to make this mess right again though. My Mum and Dad are coming to visit, and I'm scared of making Mum ill again… or worse.

I hope that you will be able to forgive me one day.

With love, Robyn.

I feel immensely better expressing these thoughts. I fold up the piece of paper and place it inside my Keats book. I don't know whether I have the guts to send it to her, or if I even need to.

Someone knocks at the door. I instantly sit up straight, suddenly alert. Grandma and Anne would've come straight in. Maybe it's Autumn, though I doubt she wants to see me, or Dean come to gloat. There's only one to find out.

"Darling!" Mum's voice floats through the smallest crack in the door as I start to open it.

"You're here early," I say before I can stop myself. "I mean, hi, Mum. I can't believe you're actually here. Come in, come in." I step back and they bustle through, carrying an overnight holdall, jackets and some plastic shopping bags. They drop everything to the floor and Mum turns to face me. She looks at me then cups my face in her hands.

"Robyn. My baby," she says. I'm crying. "You've grown up too much!"

"It hasn't been that long, Mum," I say, once again being unmasked by my tone. "Nice to see you though." She hugs me.

"Anne and Grandma went to the pool. They'll be back soon. We thought you'd take longer," I say, trying to explain the imperfect welcome I'm giving.

"Shall I put the kettle on?" Dad says, and once again the answer to everything is a cup of tea.

"Yes, please," Mum and I say at the same time. We laugh.

"We left early and there was no traffic. Couldn't believe it," Dad says filling the silence.

"That's good." I can't believe I'm being shy and awkward with my own parents. The two people who know me better than anyone.

"Been a long time since I was here," Mum says. I don't know how to talk to her. It doesn't seem real that she's here, out of hospital and on the surface of it, back to her old self. I don't want to do anything to upset that.

"I had some good news today." Might as well use what I have until Grandma comes back. "We called the college and they've said I can start. In September. With Michelle and Tanith and the others. I can do my resits in the first term, but I am allowed to start English A-Level."

"That's fantastic news, Robyn," Mum says, trying, ungracefully, to pat my arm. Dad comes over with the tea.

"I knew it would work out," Dad says, as if he had something to do with the outcome.

"All thanks to Grandma, really. She spoke to everyone and helped make my case, and asked the school to write a letter of support. She was amazing."

"That's good. I'm glad you had someone in your corner," Mum says. We sip our teas.

"Why don't we go down to the pool and find them?" Dad suggests.

"Okay," I say at the same time Mum announces she needs the toilet. While she's in there, I tidy up their bags into a neat pile at the side of the sofa. Dad washes up the cups.

"Look, Robyn," Mum says when she returns, "I know this is going to be strange for you and Anne," she has no idea, "a readjustment for you. We're not going to do everything perfectly straight away. But I want you to know

To Autumn

I'm trying my best, and I'm immensely proud of how strong and resilient you've both been."

I'm crying again. I don't know what to say. "Okay." One-word answers seem safest right now.

"Let's head over, shall we? Lead the way, Robyn. I'm not sure I could remember the route through this maze of vans," Dad says. He holds the door open for Mum and me, and I grab the spare key and lock up.

"This way," I say, barely able to remember back to when every row of mobile homes looked like a copy of the last.

"This place hasn't changed at all," Mum says.

I want to reply, "I wouldn't know because you didn't let us come here when I might have remembered it." I don't say anything though. Thankfully chlorinated shouts and screams announce the upcoming pool entrance. As we walk through the metal turnstile, a whistle trills. I stop in my tracks, causing Dad to remain stuck in the gate. I forgot Autumn could be here… except, no she won't be, will she? Because of me.

Dad bumbles into me and gently moves me to the side to give space for Mum to come through the gate. My skin burns as it seems like all eyes are on us. Grandma is sitting near the back of the pool. Anne must be in the water. We start to walk towards Grandma, and then a water-soaked bundle runs towards us and slams into Mum, hugging her with real fierceness. The pool water leaks onto Mum's shirt and linen trousers, making them see-through, but neither of them let go.

Grandma walks over to where we're standing. A few of the parents around the pool are staring at us.

"You made it!" she says, giving Dad a kiss on the cheek and waiting to say hello to Mum. When Anne finally pulls away, Grandma wraps her in a towel, then kisses Mum on the cheek as well.

"Sandra, you look well, dear," Grandma says.

"I'm getting there, Glo," Mum replies. This is the first time I'm aware of an interaction between them, even though I must've witnessed it many times when I was much younger. It's weird what brains choose to put into memories and what they leave out.

"Shall we head home and have some lunch?" Grandma asks. Why do adults think that food and cups of tea solve everything?

Chapter Twenty-five

We finish our round of cheese and tomato toasties. Mum and Dad talk about the drive up, and how clear it was and how they're glad it didn't rain. Safe subjects. My mind is a swirl, thoughts of Autumn, what Dean did, Mr Hooper, college, going home, and how it feels to see Mum again are all entangled with each other.

"Did you tell them your news, Robyn?" Grandma says, and I wonder for a second what she means. Is she trying to out me to them? Well, confirm my recently established lesbian identity to them, seeing as how they all seem to know anyway.

"She did! We're very pleased and thank you for helping her out, Mum," Dad says, filling the gap left by my confused silence.

"I finished all the word searches in the book you gave me, Dad." I wish there was more Anne could do to take the attention away from me.

"I used to love word searches," Mum says. "And that reminds me, we brought some presents with us." Mum stands up from the table and picks up the carrier bags. "I'm afraid they're all we could pick up at Exeter services." Mum opens the bag and hands a puzzle book to Anne, a paperback book of the nation's favourite love poetry for me and some shrivelled chrysanthemums to Grandma.

We say thank you and inspect our gifts. Grandma uses the water jug to hold the flowers and arranges them into a display that uplifts their appearance.

"Time for my nap, John," Mum says.

"Use my bed, dear," Grandma says. "We'll keep the noise down for you."

"Thanks, Glo, part of my new routine, I'm afraid, to help me manage the drowsiness from the medication." Mum kisses Dad and pats Anne and me on the head, then goes off to Grandma's room.

"I thought the medication didn't work for her?" I ask, in a whisper. There's still a lot we don't know. I've accepted being told the bare basics all this time, but now we need to know the details, if there's an impact on our everyday life.

"Well, it didn't work on its own," Dad says, in a serious whisper of his own. "The treatment is complicated."

"I think we can handle the details, Dad. We've handled everything else this year." My harshness surprises me.

"Why don't we clear away the dishes first," Grandma steps in.

"No, that's okay, Mum. The girls have a right to know. Robyn's right, they have done incredibly well to manage, especially when I was scarcely there for them." Perhaps the reason I've been feeling this impending doom about Mum and Dad's visit isn't just about facing up to my own mistakes. It's also time for us to stop pretending nothing happened.

"I told you that Mum had to have a course of EST – electric shock therapy. Well, that helped reset the chemical imbalance, which in turn helped Mum work with the psychiatrist to understand what went wrong in the first place, what triggered the chemicals to misbehave," Dad continues.

"You don't have to patronise us," I say, ready to be told the truth. That I'm what triggered the chemical imbalance.

"In order to stop another imbalance from happening, your Mum has to take medication, quite strong tablets, that help keep chemicals at the right levels, even if something happens that would normally trigger a spike. But the meds have side effects, one of which is drowsiness, or tiredness. Other side effects like nausea are managed by taking other tablets. She'll have to take around ten a day, every day, for a while to come." Have I done this to her? For the third time today, tears flood out of me. She has to take ten tablets a day to be able to cope with me fancying women. I need to tell her I've spent all summer putting that part of me away. She doesn't need to worry about that anymore.

"She doesn't need to do that! I'll make sure she's not triggered again," I say, my voice rising above the whisper.

"Robyn, dear," Grandma says, taking my hand, "this is not your responsibility."

"That goes for you both," Dad adds. "It's our job to look after you, not the other way around."

"We can just be normal with her?" Anne asks.

I've been too scared to ask this question. I don't know if we're supposed to be extra nice or act as though nothing happened.

"Absolutely," Dad replies, but is he convincing us or himself?

†

Mum surfaces less than an hour after she went down. We all sit around the living room, uncomfortably silent. Even Grandma doesn't have something to say.

"Your dad tells me you both made friends here," Mum says, cutting through the silence. "I'd like to hear about what you've been up to."

No, I don't think you would. I'm pretty sure being normal does not include being gay or causing someone to be fired. "Why don't you show me round, Robyn. It's been far too long since I've been here, I've forgotten where everything is. We can have a gossip." Mum has never asked me to gossip with her before.

"Let's go for a walk," I say, grateful to do something and leave the awkwardness behind for a while.

We start towards the playground. I want to steer us to the beach where it'll be easier to avoid anyone I don't want to bump into. It's weird walking past a place where so much has happened with the person that might be affected most by it all. We stride up the dunes, my legs now much more accustomed to the challenge compared to that first day. Mum takes my elbow and I pull her along with me.

"I've missed walking with you, Robyn, and swimming. Everything that I took for granted," Mum says. I don't like thinking of her missing us as much as we missed her.

"Grandma doesn't have the same motivation as you, that's for sure. She takes a lot more encouragement, but she has been really good at making sure we could still do things like that."

"I'm glad you've had the chance to connect with her, you two are alike in many ways. We should have made the effort to spend time with her sooner, and not waited until it could have been too late." I don't understand why we are still skating around the subject. Dad has updated us, I know why Mum was depressed; surely we can say the words now?

"I think we missed out, not spending time with her sooner," I reply, hoping not to upset Mum.

"Well, that's my fault," Mum says. "I put my own feelings first and should have worked harder to deal with those so that you two didn't miss out." I don't respond. If I agree with her, I'm blaming her, if I disagree then I'm lying.

"I wanted to talk just the two of us, Robyn," she continues. Here it comes. Why everything else that's wrong is my fault. "Now we understand why I became unwell, I want to try and explain it to you. You're old enough to understand," and the cause, "and I owe you some answers."

We walk onto the sand, our feet sinking with each step, but the water is too cold to walk barefoot at the shoreline. The beach has cleared out a lot today, as families start to travel home in time for kids to remember they'll be going back to school next week.

"Just after New Year, I missed a period." Definitely not what I am expecting to hear. "After a few more weeks it still hadn't come, and then my body started to feel the way it did when I was pregnant with you and Anne. Things like soreness, tiredness. I don't know if you remember last time, but I was also quite moody." I nod. She takes a breath and continues, "Well, those symptoms might indicate pregnancy." Mum was pregnant? "That's what your dad and I thought, anyway. And it was a shock, as we'd agreed a long time ago not to have any more children, because, well because my body and brain don't seem very good at managing the hormonal changes."

Despite her explanation, I know I'm still not hearing the full truth, now that Grandma has told me what happened when Mum gave birth to Anne.

"Your dad and I, we'd been discussing making the decision not to have more children permanent by him having, you know... the procedure men can have. However, by the time I missed my period, he hadn't yet had it. I was furious. I didn't want to be pregnant. I'd worked too hard to regain my mental health after the post-natal depression to let it become unstable again."

"So, what happened? You lost the baby? And that made you crazy?" I ask. I really need to find a way for my brain to intervene before words come out of my mouth.

"We're supposed to call it mentally unwell, Robyn. However, no, that's not what happened. I was starting to spiral. We went to see Dr. Patel to talk about the situation and explore our options. She did a pregnancy test, and it turned out I wasn't pregnant."

"But you..."

We stop to walk around a sandcastle being built.

"Had all the symptoms. Yes. Dr Patel did some blood tests, and they showed I was perimenopausal. That's why my period didn't come, that's why I was being moody, why parts of my body ached, why I was tired. I should have been relieved, but instead I started to spiral further. It appears my body and brain can't cope with any kind of hormone change. Dr Patel told me that perimenopause can last for years, especially as it was an early start for mine. I panicked at the idea I might be feeling like that for years, it sounded much worse than a pregnancy."

She stops walking and faces me. It's much easier to talk like this when we don't have to face each other. I can forget she's Mum.

"That was the weekend I accidentally burst in on you and Beth." The words fall between us and onto the sand.

To Autumn

Chapter Twenty-six

"Why didn't Dad tell us this?" I shout, causing a family to the left of us to stare.

"Let's turn back," Mum says, turning her body. I'm frozen, unable to make any part of my body move.

"I don't know. I have hardly any memory of what happened once I crashed the car. I was under sedation and then on strong drugs, right up to when they started the EST. He's not good at talking about women's bodies."

I feel like a volcano gearing for eruption. "You mean, all this time, I've thought it was my fault you attempted suicide because Dad was too embarrassed to tell us you're in menopause?"

"Robyn!" Mum takes hold of my arms. "Why on Earth would you think this is your fault?"

"Because. Because after you saw me and Beth kissing, you drove your car into a brick wall." I shake free and run off. I don't want to have this conversation anymore.

I arrive back at the mobile home, but it's empty. Mum enters not long behind me.

"Robyn, darling, you've done nothing wrong."

"Then why did Dad send us away?" I try not to shout again, still worried I'll trigger Mum.

"He said to me that he didn't think he was capable of looking after you two during the holidays and wanted you to be in the place he always felt safest."

"It wasn't a punishment?" I ask, wanting to be absolutely certain.

"Of course not! Is that what you've been thinking this whole time?" Mum asks. I nod, starting to feel very stupid.

"He, we, wanted to make sure you'd be looked after. It's my fault. My illness took us away from you when you needed us the most."

I sit back on the sofa. A horrible truth sinking in. Everything is upside down. Nothing that's gone down since Mum went to hospital needed to have happened. I've hurt everyone I care about, including myself, trying to protect someone who didn't need protecting.

Anne jumps through the entrance and runs to hug Mum. "You're back!" she says. "We went to the shop and

To Autumn

Dad bought me some sweets and then we booked a table for dinner tonight."

"Sounds like you've been busy," Mum says.

Dad and Grandma arrive home. Anne offers us all a sweet from the paper bag.

"Are we going to the club house as well? If I recall, that's Grandma's favourite place."

"Not on a Friday," Anne says. "She doesn't like disco night."

"Maybe we can go tomorrow, instead," Grandma says. "Have a nice walk?"

"It was okay," I say, unable to hide my grumpiness.

†

We set off together for the restaurant. The sun is already low on the horizon. I can't believe what a difference a handful of weeks makes to bring that sense of the end of summer even though it's still just about August. I shiver in the breeze.

Dad holds the door open for us all. Leo-Bradley seats us and hands out the menus, although Anne and I don't need them anymore. The items are blazed into our minds from too many visits here. Thankfully the Jacksons aren't here tonight, and there aren't many other diners at all.

"Quiet tonight," Grandma says when Leo-Bradley takes our order.

"A lot of families left today, to try and beat the traffic. The weekend will be a nightmare on the roads, end of the summer holiday and all that."

"That makes sense," Dad says. He always tries to be the expert on anything to do with traffic and directions. "I noticed it was busier coming the other direction when we drove down this morning."

We eat our meals without much fuss, I think we are all exhausted from a long and emotional day. Grandma and Dad argue about who is going to pay the bill, both of them wanting to cover it. In the end they agree to split it. After coffees for the adults and hot chocolates for Anne and me, we stand up to leave. I open the door for everyone this time, and just as I am closing it behind me, Autumn is coming towards the restaurant. The others have already started walking ahead of me, and I know I ought to be following behind. I don't even know if I'm allowed to speak to Autumn. She raises a hand in a subtle wave hello. I do the same then run to catch up with my family before they realise I'm not with them.

"Was that one of your friends?" Dad asks, putting an arm around my shoulder. I wriggle away without being obvious.

"Sort of."

Back at home, I yawn in a dramatic way and see myself off to bed. I replay Autumn's wave over and over. She didn't look angry at me. If anything, her mouth was

To Autumn

turned into a smile rather than a frown. If I was her, I'd hate me.

†

I must have fallen asleep as soon as I pulled the blankets over me last night, I didn't even hear Anne come into bed. It's early, about 6.30am I'd guess as the sun hasn't fully risen yet. Mum and Dad's snoring makes me reluctant to go for a wee even though I'm bursting. I'll opt to try and doze off again for a bit, rather than wake them up in the dawn light.

The light is streaming in when I open my eyes again. The snoring has stopped. I dash to the bathroom and try to flush as softly as I think I can. Back in the lounge, Mum and Dad are stirring. I decide to go for a shower while everyone is still waking up. I collect my towel and wash bag, and some clothes for the day. I ease the bedroom door shut behind me.

"Put the kettle on, Rob," Dad says. I fill it and flip on the switch, then ease out of the lounge door. I haven't been awake this early all summer. There's a stillness, like even the air is still asleep.

I'm the only person at the shower block, and I take the chance to enjoy a longer shower. I wash everywhere twice, keeping my hand pressed on the tap. I dry and dress and when I'm brushing my hair some other guests arrive. I give my hair one final rub of the towel and then set it on my shoulders around my neck to stop the wet curls dripping onto my shirt while I'm walking up to the caravan.

From a few rows away, I can see the door is open, which hopefully means that they are all up and about. Mum, Dad and Grandma are talking, and as I approach their muffled voices turn into fully formed words. I hear someone say my name, and step to the side, out of direct view line of the door, and listen in.

"Look, maybe I should have intervened sooner, but I really thought it was just a crush," Grandma says.

"Do you think she wanted it to happen?" Mum asks.

"All I know is, she was insistent that Autumn isn't in trouble over it."

"Have they spoken, since Mr Hooper talked to you?" Dad asks.

"Not as far as I know," Grandma replies. "I'm sorry, but I thought I should tell you."

I make some noise and yell hello to announce my return.

"I had a shower, I was awake early," I say. Stick to the easy facts.

"You were gone a while," Dad says. "And Anne's not up yet. Fancy a tea?" The answer to life, the universe and everything. Maybe Douglas Adams was wrong about the number 42.

"Yes please. What's the plan for today?" My insides are shaking.

"I think the day might be a pretty boring one. We need to go into Exeter and buy Anne's new school clothes and stationery supplies for you both. Is that okay?" Dad asks.

To Autumn

I nod. Sounds like a good distraction.

†

No one mentions that Autumn is not performing at the club house tonight, thank goodness. We settle into the booth and wait for Mr Hooper to start the show.

"This hasn't changed a bit, has it?" Mum says.

If times were different, I might have laughed.

"Apart from the big refurbishment," Grandma explains, "but I think they were keen to retain the original essence of the place." That is one way of putting it.

Mr and Mrs Jackson, with Jamie, but thankfully no Dean, enter and walk towards us. What if Dean told them as well?

"You must be Robyn and Anne's parents," Mrs Jackson says, and Grandma introduces everyone. "Our children have been playing together most of the summer, we own a mobile home at the park, too."

"Yes, we've heard a lot about you," Dad says. "I'm glad the girls made some nice friends."

"We're off back to Coventry tomorrow," Mr Jackson says to Dad. "But I hope that we'll see you all here next summer! Hope you travel home safely." Jamie waves to Anne and they turn around to try and find a table.

The lights dim, and the stage lights come on, announcing the start of the evening.

"They were Dean's parents?" Dad says to me. "Where is he, then?"

"How would I know?" I snap back.

"That was uncalled for, Robyn," Dad says. "You're not too old to be told off." The lid that has been holding down the build up of angry pressure inside me flies off, releasing bubbling steam that I can't control.

"Really? You think I need to be told off? Am I the one who has kept secrets and withheld information from people that might have been really useful for them to know? That might have prevented a big, complicated mess unfolding?"

"What are you talking about?" Dad says.

"Ssh, Mr Hooper's about to start," Grandma says.

"I've been trying to wish away a big part of myself because I thought I was protecting Mum. We've missed out on years of having Grandma in our lives, all because you're crap and keep things from us." The band arrive on stage and begin their tune up. "Phillip Larkin was right." I stand up. "Leave me alone." My head is pulsing, I need fresh air. "Don't follow me," I say, right as Mr Hooper welcomes everyone, and then I run.

I push through the double doors into the hallway which is, thankfully, empty. The band start up and the music echoes off the stark walls. I'm hot and stuffy, sweating. I turn towards the exit, finding it hard to breathe. I reach the door and pull it open, a welcome blast of cool air sweeps over me. I step out and to the left, into the shadow, and lean back against the wall of the building. I slide down, until I am sitting on the floor, still finding it hard to catch my breath.

To Autumn

"Count to four when you breathe in, count to five when you let it out," that too familiar voice says. "Slow your breathing down, if you can." She sits down next to me and waits patiently. I follow her instructions and after a minute, my breathing is slowing down and starting to return to normal.

"How did you know what to do?" I ask in a whisper when my breath allows me to talk again.

"I'm a lifeguard. I save lives, you know," she says, gently. "What happened?"

"I don't want to talk about it."

"I see. Was that your folks I saw you with last night?"

How is this not talking about it?

"Mmm." I close my eyes and keep breathing in the slow rhythm. The warmth of her on my side isn't enough to stop me shivering in the dark.

"Come with me," she says. "Don't worry, I won't make you talk." She stands up and offers a hand. I hesitate. I want to take it and to follow her. I should go back to my family.

"How can I refuse that offer?" I say, allowing her to pull me up off the floor. Her hand is soft against mine and sends a lightning bolt through my body.

She walks us back into the building, and for a second I think she's going to return me to the ballroom, but we walk straight past those doors. We walk further up the corridor, then Autumn takes out a key and unlocks the staffroom door.

We enter and she turns on the light, then closes the door locking it from the inside.

"I haven't given my key back yet," she says. The acknowledgement of her losing her job stings.

We sit down on the sofa. I'm careful to squeeze up against the arm so we aren't touching.

"Why did you say it was you who kissed me?" I need to know.

She leans to face me. "That little shit – sorry I know he's your friend…" I shake my head to say, not anymore, "told my manager that he saw me make the move on you. I would have had to tell them everything to explain why that's not exactly what happened. I knew how important it is for you to not be outed, and there was no way I could deny what Dean said without giving up your secret. Besides, I didn't try and stop you, did I? I'm as much to blame, and I did know the rules." I'm taken aback. She twists away, no longer facing me.

"You wanted to protect me? Why?" I fold my leg under me and turn to face her.

"You had a lot to lose, much more important stuff than a summer job. I care about you." Words I would have given anything to hear and words that destroy me. She cares about me. How do I tell her that it turns out I didn't need to hide my gayness and that none of this needed to have happened?

"I had a fight with Mum and Dad. That's why I was outside."

"I'm sure they'd be thrilled to know you're with me," she says, letting out a little shallow laugh. "Did Mr Hooper tell your grandma about the kiss?"

"Yeah. He came over and asked me, in front of Grandma, if it was true and whether I'm okay. Obviously, I said I am. I wanted to tell them what really happened. I'm truly sorry. I've done everything wrong, and I've hurt people I care about."

"You were doing what you thought was right," Autumn says to me, without a trace of anger or sarcasm.

"What I thought was right was actually wrong, though. That's why I had a fight with Mum and Dad tonight."

"I saw they were here. That's good your mum's doing better, I mean well enough to come here, right?" I realise that in sweating my stuff, I've forgotten the bigger picture. I did all of this because I wanted Mum to recover and be well again, and she is. Does it matter that her illness had nothing to do with me?

"Is this where I'm supposed to say the ends justify the means?" I joke.

"Do you want a cuppa–" Autumn starts to ask.

"No! I never want to drink tea again," I say, feeling silly. "Is there something else?"

"I'm sure there's some hot chocolate knocking around somewhere," she says and stands up. "We can stay here for as long as you need to cool off."

"I found out some interesting things in the last few days. If they hadn't all been keeping things from me, I don't think any of this would have happened," I say, wondering what a difference knowing the truth about Mum's previous mental ill health and Grandma and Di's relationship would have made.

"None of it?" Autumn busies herself making two hot chocolates.

"Grandma had a long-term female partner. My Aunty Di. I always thought she was Grandma's sister, but it turns out they were a couple. I'm not sure that means she's like us, not completely anyway, but she and Di and Dad were a rainbow family."

"Wow! Gloria, eh? Cool." Autumn brings the drinks over and hands a large mug to me. Our fingers brush and the contact sparks a frisson.

"And this isn't the first time Mum's been ill. Apparently, she had awful post-natal depression when Anne was born, and I stayed here with Grandma while Mum was in hospital. I was wrong about why she tried… to hurt herself." Talking about these things with Autumn is helping to make sense of them. I can't believe I can be this honest with her.

"That's a lot of emotional stress you didn't even know you had," she says. "I thought I had it bad with parents who would prefer it if I wasn't a lesbian."

I sip on the hot chocolate. My body sinks into the sofa and my eyelids start to feel heavy. I'm a deflating balloon. I close my eyes for a second…

†

The TV is on. The news. A reporter is talking about a big car accident, fragments of sentences float in and out. If there's a TV then I'm not at home, in my bunk bed. I pat my body and the space around me. I'm still wearing my clothes from last night. I reach farther and there's a leg next to me, not my own. I open my eyes. I'm still in the staff room! Autumn is asleep on the sofa next to me, our legs meeting in the middle. The light is off, but the TV is definitely on. I blink a few times and try to find my focus. There's a breaking news alert across the screen, and updates scrolling along a ticker. My brain is taking too long to catch up and read it. I blink a few more times and then see. This has to be a joke. I try and rouse Autumn, although the goosebumps on my skin aren't from touching her but from the news on the screen.

"Autumn," I say.

"Hmmm?"

"Wake up," I urge.

"What's going on? What time is it?" She takes my hand and holds it.

"Please, look at the TV." I can't bring myself to say the words of what I've seen on the screen. She starts to sit upright, still holding my hand.

"You can turn it off if you want," she says.

"No, look." I point to the screen. She reads the news ticker and watches in the pictures, double taking just as I had.

"Is this real?" she says.

"I think so, we're on BBC one."

"Then Princess Diana is dead. Shit."

To Autumn

CHAPTER TWENTY-SEVEN

Everything I've been keeping tight inside comes flooding out of me. I'm shuddering with tears and snot and sobs. Autumn doesn't say anything, she just holds me. I'm crying for Diana, but I'm also crying for all the events of the year. I could have been watching my Mum on the news back in April. The startling similarity of their accidents doesn't escape me. The guilt I'm feeling that I'm glad Mum didn't end up the same way when she very easily could have, is unsettling. In fact, she escaped with barely any physical injuries.

I need to go back to the mobile home. They'll probably be worried about me. I didn't mean to stay the whole night here. I sit up and wipe my face with my sleeve, not caring how it looks.

"I have to go home, they'll be worried," I say.

"Yes, you should be with your family. Would you like me to walk you there?" Autumn asks, and she wipes a stray tear from my cheek.

"I would like that, but I don't quite know how I would explain it. Maybe I should go on my own?" I can't believe I am saying no to spending more time with her.

"I understand," she replies. "I think you'll be okay, Robyn." I love it when she says my name.

"Let's hope so. Thank you for…" I don't know how to put into words what I am thankful for.

"You're welcome." She hugs me, our cheeks touching as we move in towards each other. As we pull apart, she kisses my forehead. "I'd better let you go."

"When are you leaving?" I wonder if this is the last time I'll see her.

"Tomorrow. Don't worry, I'll find you before I go."

†

I have about five minutes, as I walk back home, to pull myself together and figure out what I'm going to say to them all. Even though the sun has barely risen, people are up and about, whispering in hushed voices to each other. A million words bounce around my brain, and it feels like a lottery draw, wondering which will be the first plucked out.

To Autumn

The door of the mobile home is open. Mum is smoking a cigarette outside, pacing up and down.

"Where the hell have you been, young lady?" she says, as soon as she sees me, then she stubs out the cigarette and runs over to hug me. It's been ages since I smelt that familiar cloak of smoke. She pulls us apart and is about to start again, when the lottery machine in my brain releases the winning balls.

"Diana died," I say, as if this is an answer.

"Who's Diana?" Mum asks.

"Princess Diana. She died in a car crash in Paris, a few hours ago."

"Don't be silly love. Royalty don't die in car crashes. Why would you say that?" Mum is confused. Dad and Grandma come to the door of the mobile home.

"You'll wake Anne," Dad says. "And where have you been? Don't try and change the subject." I'm surprised how quickly things between us are returning to normal, after nearly six months of being handled with cotton wool.

"Princess. Diana. Died. In. A. Car. Crash. In Paris, early this morning. I'm not lying. I saw it on the news. I was with Autumn, in the staff breakroom."

"Why don't we all go back inside?" Grandma says. All around us, lights are being switched on and people are coming outside.

"Have you heard?" they say to each other.

My Keats lies open on the coffee table. The letter I wrote to Autumn, unfolded, next to it. Maybe I won't need to say anything at all. My truth has preceded me.

"I'll wake Anne," Grandma says, "we should go to the rec room and see if the TV's on there."

"This is why you need to have one in here," Dad says.

"Nonsense, I've never needed one before. Di was the one who watched…" Grandma starts crying. Anne comes out of our bedroom.

"What's going on? Robyn's back!" She comes over to hug me. "Why is everyone crying if Robyn's back?"

"Well, sweetie, Robyn told us that something unexpected has happened. We're going to head over to the complex to see if we can find out more information." Dad says.

"What is it?"

"We think that Princess Diana died in a car crash last night," Mum replies, putting her arm around Anne.

"How does Robyn know?" Anne asks.

"Long story," I say. "Come on, let's head to the Rec room."

"But we're all in our pyjamas," Anne says.

"I don't think it matters when something like this happens."

They throw on a jumper each, a dressing gown for Grandma, and their shoes. I step outside while I wait for them. More and more caravans have opened up and people are gathering in clusters. Some are already heading to the club house.

"We're not the only ones going over there," I say.

†

There's a bottleneck of people entering the building. We wait at the same spot Autumn found me last night. Groups of people shuffle in. The ballroom is open, and people are going inside.

"They've put a TV on in there," someone in front of us says. When we finally make it in, there are no seats left, meaning we have to stand at the back of the room. The small TV from the break room is playing. The same news feed from the BBC is on, only there's daylight behind the reporter this time. Some of the holiday park staff are handing out polystyrene cups of tea and coffee.

Mr and Mrs Jackson, Jamie and Dean arrive. They beeline for us, as there's hardly any space elsewhere in the room. Dean stays to the other side of his family to keep away from me. I don't have any energy to be angry anymore though. I know why he reported Autumn, he was hurt and jealous.

When the news cycle starts to repeat itself, we all become a bit fidgety.

"Let's go back and have some breakfast," Dad says. We say goodbye to the Jacksons, and manoeuvre through the crush of people. Mr Hooper steps up onto the stage and clears his throat.

"In light of this tragedy, we've decided to hold a minute's silence at 7pm tonight, here. If you want to join us, you are all welcome." He steps down from the stage, and this spurs more families to stir and begin to leave. The Jacksons are behind us.

I hang back and take my moment to catch Dean. With the crowd, he isn't able to run away from me.

"Look," I say, "I know what you did. I think I know why you did it. I was really mad, but this isn't a time to be angry anymore. I'm sorry I lied to you, that wasn't cool. I thought I was doing the right thing, but it wasn't fair."

"Oh," he says.

†

Dad takes charge of the kitchen. I change out of my clothes that I've been wearing all night. I bring in one of the garden chairs to sit at the table, there's not quite enough room in the booth for all of us at the same time.

"We found your letter to Autumn," Mum says to me, quietly. "We only read it in case it could help us find you," she continues, raising her hands in surrender. "I'm glad we did read it, because now I understand what you've been going through, darling girl."

I'm caught off guard, because I've been expecting a reprimand and punishment.

"Not that we aren't still angry you disappeared like that," she says.

"I didn't mean to be out all night. I was just talking to Autumn. She found me right after I left you all, and I fell asleep. I was going to come home, I promise." I hope my defence is good enough.

"I think we need a policy of total honesty from now on," Mum says, "from you and also from your dad and I." I nod. "So, if you are telling the truth," I nod to say I am, "then we'll forget about it. This time. It can't happen again."

"Thank you!" I am blindsided by this outcome.

"Is there anything else you want to tell us?" Mum says.

"No, everything's there in the letter." What a cop out. "I mean, if you read the letter then you know I do like Autumn…and it wasn't her that kissed me, it was the other way around. She took the blame to protect me, because she knew I wanted to protect you." I speak really quickly to stop having to think about the discomfort of saying these things. "I only found that out last night, the bit about her taking the blame."

"Why did you think I wouldn't be okay with you being gay?" I can't believe Mum says this totally casually.

"Bacon sarnies are up," Dad calls, "come and get them." We take a sandwich and serviette and sit at the table. Anne dollops a massive pile of ketchup on hers, splashing the table with it.

"Gross," I say.

We eat in an echo of silence. The park is quieter than normal, no constant murmur of kids shouting and people walking by. I'm sad this is the last bacon sandwich we'll have here.

"Right, Anne and I will do the washing up this morning," Grandma declares. Subtle. They load up the bowl and Anne carries the sponge and tea towel.

"See you in a while, crocodiles," Grandma says. They step out. I move over to the sofa.

"I thought that you didn't want me to be a lesbian and that's why you tried to commit suicide." If Mum wants honesty, honest I will be. Mum and Dad join me on the sofa.

"Oh, my love. Of course not! We love you no matter who you love. It takes a lot more than that for either you or Anne to rattle me," Mum says. She's not angry.

"I know that now. But when it happened, when you crashed the car, it was right after you found me kissing Beth, and then you threw her out, which is why I made a connection between the two situations." The concrete block that's been living in my stomach for months is shrinking with each honest statement I make.

"I wanted her to leave because I wasn't feeling well. I'm truly sorry I wasn't able to make that clear to you. I was in a very bad way at that point."

"Oh," I say. Dad puts his hand on Mum's knee. "I wish I'd known that." I stop there, not wanting to sound like I still blame Mum for my bad GCSE results and how I handled things with Dean and Autumn.

"Do you think you might be ready to let the holiday park management know the truth about the kiss with

Autumn?" Dad says. "We would support you and help you explain why you felt you had to lie about it, and why Autumn wanted to cover for you."

"Will that mean she won't be fired anymore?" I ask.

"I don't know, but I think it will go a long way to helping her get her job back." Dad gives me a little bit of hope. I have a chance to do the right thing, and I want to take it.

"Good. How are you feeling? You've had a big twenty-four hours," Mum asks.

"I'm not sure there's a word that could describe it. Exhausted, relieved, sad, happy. Worried," I answer.

"What are you worried about?" Mum asks.

"What's happened to Diana, it reminds me of what happened to you. It makes me worried that could happen again, only with a different outcome." It feels much better to be able to express all of this, rather than bottle it up out of worry I'll be making things worse.

"I think this event reminds us that nothing is certain," Mum says, not actually helping me, "but I can promise you I am doing everything I can to keep recovering and to stay well. And we now have a crisis plan in place, which means if I do start to feel unwell again, everyone knows what to do to help me."

"That sounds good," I say.

"I hope you can trust us. Please believe that we want to do everything we can to make sure you and Anne are safe and happy," Dad says.

"Does that mean we can see Grandma more often? Can we come back and visit?" I couldn't imagine these words coming out of my mouth at the start of the summer. I like it when things surprise us by turning out better than we expected.

"Absolutely. We should have done that years ago," Dad says.

"Are we going to the minute's silence tonight? I'd like to be there," I ask.

"Of course, whatever you want. It'll be nice to do that as a family. It seems like everyone is affected by the news," Mum says. "Are you ready to talk to the management? I think you are very brave for doing that."

"I'm just telling the truth, which I should have done all along," I say. "Maybe we can tell Mr Hooper though. He was the person that talked to me and Grandma."

"Telling the truth can sometimes be the hardest thing to do," Mum says.

†

There're too many people to gather inside the club house. Instead, we form a clumsy circle outside instead, dusk wrapping us all up in a blanket. Someone lights a candle. Mr Hooper moves to the middle, and a hush falls.

"Let us spend a few minutes in quiet reflection on the loss of our People's Princess, a mother and champion for many vulnerable people, a role model. Her death reminds us that loss and grief are natural parts of life. Rest in peace,

To Autumn

Princess Diana." Perfect words from Mr Hooper. A few of the crowd mumbles "rest in peace" with him.

I feel a tug on my little finger. I turn to my left to see Autumn standing slightly behind me. She brushes her hand against mine, our little fingers intertwining. Sharing the silence with all the people I love and other people at the park is powerful. After too short a time, Mr Hooper announces a thank you and people start to leave around us. I turn around ready to say "hello" to Autumn, but she has disappeared.

Chapter Twenty-eight

I sleep well for the first time in days. I wake up excited for a Monday morning. The heaviness of all the secrecy and stress is lifting off me, and my body feels decompressed. All my muscles and organs have room to breathe at last. The concrete block in my stomach has dissolved.

Of course, I'm also feeling a tinge of sadness. It's strange when competing feelings contend for attention. The death of a person who seemed like they should live forever, who was a symbol of hope in the world, is not just a shock. It's bigger than that. We all felt that pain together, yesterday at the minute's silence.

To Autumn

I lie dozing in the bunk, the penultimate time I'll be waking up here. A crack of light sneaks in under the window blind. The sounds of Mum and Dad trying to move about quietly drift in and out. I wonder what our final day at the holiday park will hold.

†

There's a blissful breeze while we finish off breakfast in the lounge, a sign that summer is ending. Autumn knocks on the open caravan door. She's carrying a bulging bag.

"G'day," she says.

"Come in, dear," Grandma says. I freeze. My worlds are colliding. "This is the famous Autumn," Grandma says to Mum and Dad, as if it wasn't obvious.

"Nice to meet you, Mr and Mrs Gale," Autumn says, her down-under cadence as lyrical as ever. She hovers at the door.

"We've heard a fair bit about you!" Dad says. Trying to be funny, perhaps? Making me cringe, instead.

"Can I have a minute alone with Robyn please?" This is the moment where she tells me she wishes she'd never met me, that I've ruined her life, asks for her mix tape back, has decided to fly home and finish uni in Melbourne instead of Exeter.

I follow her out of the door, down the two concrete steps to the white plastic garden set that lives mostly unused under our kitchen window. I don't think there's that much privacy between here and inside, and I'm sure they'll all be able to hear her scolding me. I deserve it, I've managed to mess up her life almost as much as my own.

"Thank you for explaining what really happened between us. To Mr Hooper and the others."

That wasn't the opening I was expecting. "I should say 'My pleasure' but…"

"I imagine it was a hard thing to do. That said, it made a difference, Robyn. I've been invited back to work next summer, as a lifeguard and occasional entertainer. But they've given me the rest of the season off." She smiles.

I let out a huge sigh. "You mean I haven't ruined your life as well?"

"No one's life is ruined, is it? You were brave and vulnerable and told your truth, even though you thought you had something to lose." She's giving me way more credit than I deserve.

"I waited until the stakes were a little lower," I rebut. "I could've done it much sooner."

"Maybe ever-so-slightly earlier, but you were honest when it was a hard thing to be. Without anything bad happening. Good things happening, in fact. I wish I'd been able to be more truthful with my parents when I was coming out." She finishes speaking and we sit quietly for a few moments.

"Would you like a drink?" I ask, realising I've been rude not to offer. At the same time, Autumn lifts up the bag she brought. "So, I know you'll be going home in a few days. I…have a gift for you." Another gift?

"You already gave me a birthday present," I say, wondering what's in the bag and why I deserve this kindness.

"I know, you dingo, but I've been feeling guilty about something," she says.

"You've been feeling guilty? You haven't done anything to feel guilty about." I've been wallowing so much in my own guilt and problems, I haven't stopped to think about anyone else's complicated feelings.

"I'm glad you see it that way," she says, "but I don't. When you stopped coming to watch *Neighbours* with me, I felt awful. I was out of line, making assumptions about you without asking whether you were okay with that."

"Sure, but I am a lesbian. You were right with your assumption," I say, confused.

"Yes, but I also assumed you were cool with it, and that I could be open about it with you, when you weren't ready for that. For quite good reasons, I think. I should have been more sensitive. I know what it's like to realise that about yourself. It's not a straightforward process, even when families do accept it." Her voice is shaking. This is the first time I'm seeing her not be totally cool, calm and collected.

"You can say that again," I say. She lets out a small, throaty laugh.

"I actually have two things for you," she continues. "Firstly, I want you to know, I did break up with Hayley. That day when your Gran drove us to the station, I'd ended it. I wanted to tell you in the car, but obviously I couldn't."

I think back to that moment. How frustrated I was with Grandma for offering them the ride, how awkward and uncomfortable I was, squashed in the back with them.

"It wasn't pretty. She was very upset, and I'll probably have to face bumping into her on campus for the next two years, but I couldn't stay in a relationship when I'd started to fall for someone else."

I picture her coming face to face with Hayley and Hayley forgiving her, and them making up, and kissing.

"And secondly, these," she continues, handing the bag to me. Inside are five VHS tapes, all neatly labelled, *Neighbours* and a date range. "I taped all of the episodes for you. All twenty-three of them. So, you won't miss a single one. I can't have the only other superfan I know breaking her record of watching every episode because of me."

This might be the greatest gift of all time.

"For real?" I am stuck for words to convey the utter happiness I feel right now. She nods. "I don't know what to say. This is the nicest thing anyone's ever done for me. How did you manage it?"

"With a little bit of help from my friends," she says with a wink. "The guy you call Leo…We took the VCR out of the rec room, as no one ever uses it there, and hooked it up to the TV in the break room. Then I bought a stack of tapes from the market. Lucky it's on twice a day, eh? That made things a bit easier."

To Autumn

"You're amazing," I say, tears welling in the corners of my eyes. Not only is this an incredible thing for her to do for me, it's also a reminder that we'll be saying goodbye.

"Something to remember me by, when you're back in London," she says, reading my mind once again.

"I don't think I'll ever be able to forget you," I say, the honesty catching me off guard.

"You've made quite an impression on me as well, Robyn. No one else could have had me negotiating TV access with my work colleagues, every weekday for a whole summer."

The unspoken meaning that coats our words hangs in the air between us. I can't be imagining this, can I? The electricity is as strong as the first day I saw her by the pool, blowing her whistle.

I lean over and kiss her on the cheek. A less-than-subtle cough comes from behind me. Grandma appears on the steps by the door.

"We've been talking in here," she says. Uh oh. Is this going to be an intervention? "Come inside, we've put the kettle on." Of course.

I take the bag of VHS tapes, excited to have hours of watching ahead of me, one reason to look forward to going home. College doesn't start until next Monday, meaning I'll have some time to catch up this week when we're back at home. The only downside is that I'll be watching them alone.

We go inside and sit slightly apart on the sofa. I'm too scared to start the conversation, so I just sit and wait for someone else to begin.

Dad brings over some teas, and a milk jug and sugar bowl. Autumn drinks her tea black. Yuk.

"We will be driving back home tomorrow, as you know, Robyn," Dad starts, "and your grandma wants to come up to London to visit Kensington Palace and lay some flowers for Princess Diana. In the papers they've announced that the funeral will be televised at the weekend. We thought it might be nice to all watch it together. But there's not enough room in the car for all five of us plus our bags…and we don't think the Fiesta has what it takes to make it all the way to Wimbledon."

"Okay," I say. Not really anything that affects me yet.

"The point is," ah there is a point, "Mum, I mean, your grandma, is going to travel up by train on Friday."

"Oh, get to it John," Grandma jumps in. "If you like, you could stay here with me, and we can take the train together." Now they have my attention. I don't have to go home tomorrow! I smile. "Annnnnd, if we aren't being presumptuous, Autumn would be welcome to stay here in the mobile home with us. In the lounge of course."

I turn to look at Autumn, not quite computing what's being suggested. Are they saying Autumn can stay here, with me, overnight? She smiles at me, looking as surprised as I feel.

To Autumn

"I mean, that's very kind of you, Mrs. Gale," Autumn says.

"Call me Gloria, dear," Grandma says.

"Are you sure? Robyn, what do you think?" I was hoping not to have to give my opinion on this, because my heart is playing bass guitar right now.

Yes, yes, a thousand times yes. "Um, I don't know, what do you think?" I ask her.

"That sounds like two yeses to me," Grandma decides for us.

"Only if you want to," I say to Autumn.

"If you want me to, I want to," Autumn says. "We can make a start on those tapes in the break room, there won't be as many people to fight with for the TV this week."

"Haven't you already seen them?" I ask. I'm totally confused by what's happening today, everything is upside down. In a good way.

"It'll be fun to watch again with you," she says, and sounds shy but she leans over and knocks her shoulder against mine. More topsy turvy happenings.

"Looks like we have a plan then," Grandma says and looks very smug indeed. I'm happy to let her have this though.

"Well played, Glo," Mum says, giving her a high five. "It will be lovely to have you come and stay for a few days and help with the girls settling back into school and college. I think they've grown quite attached to you."

"Can she move in with us?" Anne asks. A very bold question.

"One step at a time, love," Grandma says, with a sly wink to Anne.

"Right then, we have some arrangements to settle," Dad says, clasping his hands together the way he does when he wants to get down to business. "We're leaving first thing tomorrow morning, which means, Anne, we'll have to pack up your things today. Robyn, if you pick out some clothes for the next few days, we can take the bulk of your stuff back in the car and then you won't have to lug that suitcase on the train."

"Sounds good," I say, although I'd much rather be slouching off to start watching my tapes.

"I need to go and pack up my things," Autumn says. "I'll leave you to it."

I frown a big dramatic frown. "Okay," I relent.

"I'll bring my bags over tomorrow. We'll have three whole days to plough through those tapes." It's not really the tapes I'm going to miss for the rest of the day.

"I'll hold you to that," I say, a glimmer in my eye.

"I'm counting on it," Autumn says. She leans in to hug me, then stands up. "It's been a real pleasure to meet you all, especially you, Mrs… Gloria." Grandma stands up and hugs Autumn too.

"You're a good girl," Grandma says.

"Bye, everyone, safe travels." Autumn turns to leave, then Anne rushes up and gives her a surprise hug, too.

To Autumn

"I'll see you next summer, matchstick girl." Autumn exits but turns one last time to wave at me before walking towards her digs.

Chapter Twenty-nine

We're in a taxi on the way to Newton Abbot station. I'm going to miss Grandma's mobile home and Smugglers' Cove. I could not have imagined feeling like this six weeks ago, to almost the very day, when we arrived here. How much can change in a short amount of time. That's my motto for the whole year.

Grandma has packed two suitcases just for herself. I wonder if she thinks she's moving in with us. Not that I'd complain. I hope she does stick around for a little while. We're going to Kensington Palace tomorrow. The newspaper photos show a sea of flowers already left in tribute to Princess Diana. Thousands of people have flocked to send their wishes and mourn. Grandma said she's never seen anything like it.

The taxi takes a corner too quickly and we're thrown around on the backseat, causing me to lean hard into Autumn. I grab hold of the VHS tapes as they try and escape from my bag. Even though we've spent all week watching them, plus the new episodes from this week, I won't be letting them go. One day there might come a time where I want to rewatch them.

This has been the best week of my life. For the first time in longer than I can remember, I've had nothing at all to worry about. No stress about Mum being unwell or not recovering, no stress about being gay, college all sorted and no responsibilities. At least I've had one week of the summer my teachers promised me.

The last few days have been mostly watching episode after episode of *Neighbours*, going for a swim and in the evenings playing cards with Grandma. All with Autumn and her sarcastic sense of humour by my side for pretty much every second of it. We've had late night deep and meaningfuls, covering everything from primary school bullies to big life dreams. She wants to teach English Literature. I think I want to write. She's shared more of her favourite music and books with me, and we've drawn up a movie list to watch together. I'm coming to visit her at Exeter in half term.

We haven't kissed again, yet. I think both of us want to take things slowly and enjoy getting to know each other.

The pressure is removed, knowing we don't have to be lovey-dovey and physical all the time. Besides, we've not really had a chance for any privacy, and it doesn't mean I don't want to kiss her, or that I don't think about kissing her all the time. I have a feeling she's waiting for me to make a move. We have been holding hands, though. A lot.

†

At the station, Autumn and I take the suitcases out of the boot while Grandma pays the driver. I find a trolley cart and stack most of the cases on there, this makes walking up the ramp to the platform much easier. At least it's not raining.

We're a little early, Grandma wanted to allow plenty of time. I'm not sure what she's allowing time for. Grandma trails behind us up to the platform, then decides she wants a cup of tea from the station café. Autumn and I sit on a bench on the uncrowded platform. We squash up next to each other even though there's plenty of room, her pinky finger interlinking with mine.

"If someone'd said to me six weeks ago this is how the summer would be ending, I'd have thought they were stoned," I say.

"Ditto." She smiles.

Grandma strolls back to us, precariously carrying her tea in take away cup, no sleeve.

"Well, girls, this is it. Off to London we go!" Grandma says, and far down the track the train comes into

To Autumn

view. It slowly chuffs towards us. What a different journey this will be, no Anne, no fusty old ladies, no concrete block filling my stomach. Instead, my new girlfriend-in-waiting joining us. I couldn't be happier.

Katie M Hall

AUTHOR'S NOTE

At the time of finishing the first draft of *To Autumn,* Fremantle Media announced they will be cancelling *Neighbours* after just over 37 years on TV. As you might imagine, I was devastated. However, a few months later Amazon Prime revived the show. Phew! And then, just as this book goes into production… devastation once more as cancellation is happening again. My love for *Neighbours* is evident in Robyn and Autumn's shared obsession with it. A sincere and mammoth thank you to the thousands of cast and crew who introduced me to the residents of Ramsay Street, many of whom have been almost life-long companions and a part of my daily life since I was six. From your number one fans, Katie, Robyn and Autumn.

To Autumn

You may also have noted, music and literature play a big part in the evolving connection of Robyn and Autumn. I'd like to share with you the soundtrack I had on repeat whilst writing the book, and some recommended reading based on Robyn and Autumn's discussions.

Music
"Beautiful Girl" - INXS
"Closer to Fine" – Indigo Girls
"Closer to the Stars" & "Miss This" – Soul Asylum
"Confide in Me" & "I Should Be So Lucky" – Kylie Minogue
"Constant Craving" – KD Lang
"Fade Into You" – Mazzy Star
"Hedonism" – Skunk Anansie
"I Shall Believe" – Sheryl Crow
"Love Will Tear Us Apart" – Joy Division
"Overlap (live)" – Ani Di Franco
"Torn" – Natalie Imbruglia
"Wild Horses" – The Rolling Stones
"Wonderwall" – Oasis
"Your Little Secret" – Melissa Etheridge

Books
My love of Keats began during A-Level (High School) English Lit classes, where I couldn't get enough of his poems that tried to use words to capture the feeling of unrequited love, anticipation, and the moments before the

embodied experience of real joy. I wanted this to be a connection for Robyn and Autumn to share. You might notice a number of Keats references throughout the book.

    John Keats: The Complete Poems (Penguin Classics, 1977)
    You can also explore Keats' work via the Poetry Foundation: https://www.poetryfoundation.org/poets/john-keats)
    Keats: The Letters of John Keats 1814-1821 by John Keats (Harvard University Press, 1974)
    Oranges are Not the Only Fruit by Jeanette Winterson (Pandora Press, 1985)

About the Author

KATIE M HALL is a forty-something journalist and writing lesbian Londoner. She is co-founder and former editor-in-chief of the Planet London family of websites and contributed hundreds of articles for the LBQT community including book & film reviews, celebrity interviews, opinion pieces and features between 2011 and 2015. Her writing can also be found in many issues of the UK based Diva Magazine.

Katie's poems and short stories have been shortlisted for several national UK writing awards. Her poetry is included in the Arachne Press anthologies Byways (2024) and Tymes goe by turnes (2020) and her short stories feature in various LesFic collections such as L Is For…, (2014) and LesFic Eclectic volume 2 (2020).

Katie is the creator and screenwriter of the first London LBQ web series, the award winning She's in London and producer of the award-winning indie feature Under the

Katie M Hall

Influencer (2024). Find out more at www.katiemhall.com or follow on Instagram @katiemargarethall

To Autumn

OTHER AFFINITY BOOKS

Fairytail Farm by Ali Spooner
Dr. Hill McCall and her wife Alice dreamed of developing a sanctuary for unwanted cats and dogs to live out their lives as a retirement project. Hill has secretly worked on the project for months when a wealthy benefactor surprises her with a large donation, allowing Hill to be more aggressive with the project's opening. A group home operator approaches Hill about summer volunteer positions for four girls as Fairytail Farm becomes more than just a sanctuary for the animals. It creates an environment of love and kindness for the animals and all that support the project. Several love stories develop from first love to mature couples who have found their forever person. Fairytail Farm is more than a dream come true. It is a home for happily ever afters.

The Love Demand by Annette Mori
In the dazzling realm of reality television, where love and drama entwine in a complicated dance as old as time, a groundbreaking series emerges that transcends the ordinary. *The Love Demand* is not your typical reality show. Lacey Fellows isn't sure she wants to subject herself to further humiliation, however, on the off chance her girlfriend may agree to accept a second marriage proposal, Lacey

reluctantly consents to participating in the new reality show. What she doesn't count on is meeting a kindred spirit—one she can't seem to shake from her thoughts. Jaimie would do almost anything for her girlfriend, including following her to the ends of the earth and participating in a conniving television show that puts her in front of a camera, which happens to be her least favorite place. Her girlfriend, Sabina, hasn't met a camera she doesn't like. They couldn't be more opposite, but Jaimie still hopes Sabina will want marriage, kids, and the whole shebang. The last thing she expects is to fall in love with someone else. Let the games begin.

Sullivan's Trace by Ali Spooner
Micah "Sully" Sullivan has settled into a solitary life at the family horse ranch after her father's death. When her long-term vet, Doc Barton, plans to retire, his granddaughter, Bryn, arrives to take over his practice. An attack on one of Sully's prized horses throws Sully and Bryn into a whirlwind as they fight to save the young animal. Just as Sully is becoming comfortable with her growing attraction to Bryn, tragedy occurs, and her brother and his wife are killed in an accident. Sully's solitary life drastically changes when a family of three is born.

Love Sins by Annette Mori
Jessica Green's life is predictable and boring. As the chief engineer for Solar Flair, her career is right on track. Her love life, not so much. The last thing she expects is a call from her estranged father's attorney. Too curious to ignore the message, she can't resist meeting with him and discovering more about specific instructions related to his

estate, as well as the letter her father left for her. Rattled by what she finds at her father's home, she promptly dials 911.

Special Agent Amanda Forrester is perplexed by a call to join a homicide investigation until she arrives at the scene and learns the victim is not only a serial killer but an elite assassin the authorities have been after for years. To Amanda's increasing irritation, the daughter recognizes a picture of the last target and insinuates herself into the investigation. As the case takes a surprising turn, Amanda finds she has landed smack dab in the middle of a complicated and dangerous situation. The facts lead her to a puzzle weaving together the recent suicide of a wealthy businessman with the activities of several prominent politicians. Amanda must join forces with a mysterious organization and the persistent woman she finds increasingly hard to resist. Her instinct to protect the alluring and vulnerable Jessica Green kicks into high gear, taking the reader on a roller-coaster journey for the last book in *The Next Generation* series.

A Wild Moon Rises by Jen Silver

Successful author, Malory G Holmes, has had a rough year. Wounded by an emotional breakup and writer's block she returns home after eight months travelling to discover the startling results of a DNA test. Apparently, through her mother's side, she is related to a baronet with an estate in Briarbay, Northumberland. She decides to visit the place to find out more about this unknown side of her family.

Selene Wylde is content with life, running a bookshop in the small hamlet of Briarbay. She also looks after her father, Reginald, who is grieving over the recent death of his husband, Sir Alan Guyatt. Reginald is worrying about his claim to stay at Briarbay Hall as the Will of Sir Alan has not yet been found.

With the arrival in her shop of a very attractive, well-known writer, Selene's world begins to tilt alarmingly. Malory and Selene become entangled in a web of secrets and deceptions with the added complication of a rapidly growing attraction.

The Wolf and The Unicorn by Ali Spooner (Erotica)

Ready to explore a steamy, passionate, and tantalizing erotica romance....

Keagan and Celeste have built a solid relationship on trust and independence. A successful surgeon, Keagan understands Celeste's supercharged libido and her desire to experience a variety of sexual encounters. Everything changes when Sky, a new doctor, arrives at the hospital, and Celeste is immediately drawn to the younger woman. Keagan is surprised when she is also attracted to Sky, who shares common interests with Celeste and her. When more than a physical attraction develops, the three women discover a loving relationship beyond the bedroom.

The Blank White Page by Ali Spooner

Tatum Chastain, Corporate Officer of Chastain International, her family's real estate empire, accepts the challenge her father, Charles, has set forth. Charles has tasked Tatum and her brother, Charlie, to survive in the wilderness for six months to prove their skills in taking over the family business once he retires. Charles fails to realize that Tatum would fall in love with the southeastern Alaska cabin he has chosen for her to test her resilience and creativity. Tatum prepares for life in the bush, and shortly

To Autumn

after she arrives, Poe, a beautiful raven, becomes her companion and guardian. When River Foster, a designated hunter for her village, crosses Tatum's path, she finds a different kind of love awaits her.

Affinity
Rainbow Publications

eBooks, Print, Free eBooks

Visit our website for more publications available online.

www.affinityebooks.com

Published by Affinity Rainbow Publications
A Division of Affinity eBook Press NZ LTD
Canterbury, New Zealand

Registered Company 2517228

Printed in Great Britain
by Amazon